CW00920179

POMPEII

CITY OF GAY SEX

GAY ROME SERIES

EVAN D. BERG

DISCLAIMER

Pompeii, city of gay sex: A novel is a work of fiction. All incidents and dialogue, and all characters and events are products of the author's imagination and are not to be construed as real. Any resemblance to actual persons, living or dead, events, or locales is entirely coincidental.

WARNING

Gay erotic romance. The material in this book contains explicit sexual content that is intended for mature audiences only. All characters involved are adults capable of consent, are over the age of eighteen, and are willing participants.

Published by Faliscan Publishing.
Copyright © 2024 Evan D. Berg.
ISBN Paperback: 979-8-87-853861-9.

Book One

1

I ran away. It was the only thing to do. I had no plans and nowhere to go, only a persistent desire to break free. The moment I had been waiting for so long had finally arrived, and I was not a fool to let it slip away.

My knowledge of the city helped me to wander with ease, but the heavy moonbeams were my best aid in moving fast and stealthily through the deserted midnight streets. An abandoned wooden cart with straw became the perfect shelter to get some sleep and bide my time until dawn, when I could walk to the city walls, now closed for the night. Once the gates were reopened in the morning, Neapolis would never see a trace of me again.

I awoke to the first rays of sunshine and the sounds of activity emerging in the town. A group of fishermen passed me as I was getting out of the cart. I trailed them to the tightly guarded gates, where I discreetly hid behind a corner and watched as they presented their documents to the officials, who subsequently let them out. Concealing myself in one of their boats was not an option since they were undergoing a thorough inspection.

Shortly thereafter, another party arrived—a man with a donkey cart accompanied by a few youngsters. He informed the guards that they were pomegranate pickers—a trade I hadn't been aware of. He elaborated that they were heading to work in the villas dotting the hills around the city. This is my chance, but how can I join them?

Stalking them discreetly, I emerged from my concealment and as they approached the exit I took up the last position in line. The guard doing the head count frowned when he reached me.

"Thirteen. Didn't you say you had twelve?"

The man glanced back, meeting my gaze with a raised eyebrow, as my heart pounded.

"I'm sorry, officer. I meant thirteen. I'm not quite awake yet."

The inspector nodded, his expression holding a hint of admonishment. He let us through and promptly closed the gates. *I can't believe it. I'm out, I'm free!*

I walked with the group in silence for a while. Why had that man covered for me and allowed me to join them so easily? An unpleasant sensation churned in my stomach. I picked up the pace to catch up with him.

"*Domine*, may I ask you a question?"

He scowled at me.

"Could you tell me why you didn't tell the guard that I wasn't a part of your group?"

"Don't think I didn't recognize you." His mouth curled into a twisted smile as he firmly grasped my chin. "I know who you are, and I'm going to get big money for you."

I swallowed hard. *There goes my newfound happiness.*

"Besides, an extra pair of hands is always good help."

After a lengthy walk we reached the first villa. A slave guided us to the courtyard, where the pomegranate trees were located. All we had to do was pluck the fruit and place them in baskets. *Simple enough.* Each boy chose a different tree, and we worked in silence. I glanced at the fellows around me. They all looked about my age, eighteen, with brawny arms, no doubt accustomed to strenuous labor. Their complexion bore a swarthy hue, a stark contrast to my milky white skin. My curly red hair was another feature that set me apart.

Everyone was stooping to lay the fruit in the baskets, and I was doing just that, but my back got tired quickly, and I opted for a more manageable approach—simply dropping the fruit.

"Don't do that!" the man yelled at me. "You're going to bruise the fruit, *stulte!*"

My face turned red. "I'm sorry, *domine*, it's just that I—"

"You've never picked fruit before, that's obvious."

I lowered my head.

"This is how you do it." He demonstrated what I already knew.

"I will do so, *domine*."

"You'd better."

We worked in different villas, loading basket after basket, to a point where I wasn't sure if the donkey would be able to carry so much weight. The man kept a closer eye on me. He was right to do so; I would have escaped already, had I possessed any knowledge of the surrounding terrain. My parents had never taken me beyond the city walls. A couple of vineyards in the vicinity could have provided me with shelter, but I resisted the urge to run toward them, wary of drawing the attention of individuals who might betray my whereabouts to the man. My gaze stopped on something dominating the horizon—something whose existence was always taken for granted—the proud Mount Vesuvius. The numerous tall trees covering its slopes offered a feasible option for concealment as the group proceeded to the next villa.

My captor took a few steps away from the group to relieve himself while gazing at the scenery. I walked backward quietly as the wind carried the arc of his golden stream.

"Master, master!" some of the boys shouted as I neared the edge of his sight. "The new one is trying to escape!"

"Get him!" he shouted.

I turned around and sprinted at full speed, my legs ablaze. Within moments, my lead was dwindling, and fatigue creeping in. Desperation fueled me as I circled the mountain, praying they would lose my trail. Momentarily out of their sight, my sole chance was to run uphill. Running grew increasingly challenging as the slope steepened, prompting me to hastily choose a tree to climb.

The youngsters conveyed to their master that they had lost track of me, eliciting him to unleash a barrage of insults. Cautious, I remained perched in the tree like a frightened squirrel until their voices faded with the setting sun. After descending, I contemplated the horizon for a while and then returned my gaze to the mountain. *I'm already halfway up, I should keep ascending.* I trudged uphill for an eternity, watching the lush slopes transform abruptly into a barren, grayish expanse.

Crouched low and gripping onto any accessible rock, I reached a vantage point. The summit of Mount Vesuvius had a bowl-shaped structure, a surprising fact, since from afar it looks like a cone. Stepping cautiously into the crater, I quickly withdrew as the ground beneath nearly scorched my sandals. *I've seen enough; it's time to descend.*

I wandered through the dense woods, the descending sun indicating I was moving southward. I veered off the *via Romana*, fearful of someone looking for me or of falling victim to bandits. A chill wind blew, making the hairs on my exposed skin stand on end. In my haste to escape, I did not consider the weather, but now I found myself shivering. All I had on was my tunic, my sandals, and a satchel; I lacked even a dagger to defend myself.

The forest assumed a menacing demeanor as darkness fell. The haunting hoots of owls, the eerie tweets of night birds, and the rustling chatter of countless other creatures pervaded the surroundings. Yet, nothing was as chilling as the distant howls that echoed through the air.

As I continued to walk, doubts creeped in. Maybe running away hadn't been the wisest decision after all. Now I was going to starve and freeze to death. The only thing I had to eat was a pomegranate I had stolen before fleeing the villa, but even though my stomach was growling, I kept it tucked away in my satchel, reserving it for a moment when hunger became truly unbearable.

A pair of ominous gray eyes fixed on me just a few paces away brought me out of my musings. A spine-chilling growl broke the stillness, affirming my worst fears. Carefully, I retreated, my gaze fixed on the creature. The wolf approached slowly, its growls intensifying with each step. Bumping into a tree, I leaned against it. Snapping off a branch, I brandished it at my adversary. The beast's full features were revealed in the moonlight: it was old and feeble, yet undoubtedly hungry.

The predator lunged at me, snarling with its sharp teeth bared. Reacting on instinct, I swung the branch with all the strength I could muster. The impact knocked it back, momentarily throwing its gnarled frame off balance, but resilience sparked in its eyes, and it quickly regained composure. Launching a second, more ferocious assault, the wolf melded us, human and beast, into a chaotic whirl of fur and limbs. The chirping of crickets became a mere backdrop to our grunting. Its paws tore at my clothing, scratching my skin, as my hands grappled with the sinewy strength of its aging body.

With the branch lost in the frenzy, my fingers fumbled in my satchel for the pomegranate—the sole weapon at my disposal. The wolf renewed its assault, teeth snapping inches from my face, but I seized it by the neck and wrestled it into submission. Heart pounding, I extracted the fruit and, keeping the beast firmly pinned to the ground, thrust it into its snout, forcing it into its throat with all my might. Its snarls turned into whimpers, and it soon went still. My hands trembled as I stood up; I had extinguished another being for the first time.

Hungry as I was, I pushed myself to keep walking. I could not go much further, so I scoured the surroundings for a cave, a crevice, or any semblance of shelter. A dreamlike shape appeared in the darkness, merely a small structure with a thatched roof—a palatial retreat to me. Summoning the final vestiges of my strength, I staggered toward it.

I reached the door and unlatched it. As I pushed it open, a stench of manure and the sound of horses neighing assaulted my senses. Gently petting the horses, I reassured them that I posed no threat. After they settled, I sank into the hay, succumbing to instant slumber.

The following morning, I awoke to a stick prodding my cheek. As I opened my eyes, shielding them from the sunlight with my forearm, a vision gradually emerged before me: an athletic chest covered by a sleeveless tunic, exposing sculpted, olive-skinned arms. A gently rounded face, adorned with a budding beard, and framed by short brown curls, took shape next. Almond-shaped brown eyes, brimming with curiosity, completed the enchanting image of a boy found only in blissful dreams.

"Wake up! Who are you, and what are you doing here?"

2

"Who are you, and why are you poking my face?"

"I don't need to tell you who I am. I live here."

"Where am I?"

"You haven't answered my question."

I tried to get up, but he kept me pinned down with the stick. "If you allow me to rise, I can explain everything."

He acquiesced. The ominous atmosphere had dissipated, leaving only three horses and hay bales strewn around. I peered outside through a little window and was greeted by the sight of farmland.

"You still haven't explained why you were sleeping here."

"I was walking in the forest, and the night caught me unsheltered." I paused. "Besides, a wolf attacked me." I displayed the scratches on my arms.

He looked at them unimpressed. "If a wolf had attacked you, you wouldn't have lived to tell."

"But it did!" I exclaimed, waving my arms. "It pounced on me, but I grabbed it by the neck and shoved a pomegranate down its throat."

"Is this how you grabbed it?" he asked, gripping my neck. He drew his face near mine, locking eyes. I held my gaze, refusing to blink. I didn't want him to think I was afraid, because I wasn't. His body odor fascinated me—a very pleasant blend of his own scent mixed with lavender. He let go of me.

"You're not lying. I can tell when someone is telling the truth."

"Thank you," I said, stroking my neck. "Can we go outside? I really need some fresh air."

He opened the door and walked behind me. The sun graced the sky, and a gentle breeze danced through the branches of nearby trees, as squirrels frolicked in the grass. Behind me was a large *villa rustica*, featuring commonplace, white-painted walls and fired clay roofs.

"You live there?"

"Need I remind you that I'm the one asking the questions here?"

"Sorry," I said with a smile. "It's a lovely place. So much better than the city."

"So you come from the city."

I remained silent. *Here I am, revealing more than I should.*

"Pompeii?" he asked, arching an eyebrow.

"Uh, no. Another city."

"Neapolis?" He stared at me for a few more moments. "Look at your skin; you're the palest kid I've ever seen. I like your hair, though. Reddish blond, not very common in these parts. How old are you?"

"I just turned eighteen this month."

"I'm nineteen."

We fell into a brief silence.

"I think I should take you to my parents," he finally said. "Maybe they'll be able to get more out of you."

He walked toward the villa, and I followed him, already feeling a certain closeness to him.

"My name is Lucius, by the way."

"I'm Renatus."

A few minutes later, we passed through an arched gate covered with vines that opened into a central courtyard, its perimeter colonnaded on three sides with columns of red and white stucco. To its sides were grape and olive pressing rooms.

The inside of the villa reflected a practical working farm rather than a lavish estate like the ones I had worked on the previous day. Nevertheless, an intriguing quality to its simplicity pervaded the air.

"Mom? Mom, come here!" Renatus' voice resonated through the empty stucco walls of the atrium. "I want you to meet someone."

"Who is it?"

A tall white woman emerged, draped in a dark green robe, drying her black hair with a towel. She was of a fuller figure, her age appeared to be around forty-five and, despite lacking the airs of a high society lady, she exuded a sense of refinement.

"He's my friend Lucius. I met him in the barn; he was sleeping there with the horses."

His friend. He just called me his friend. My heart raced like a drum.

"You can tell," she said, wrinkling her nose. "Why don't you take your friend to the bath first?"

Her tone held a hint of sternness but wasn't unfriendly. Perhaps she was simply a bit bothered to have a stranger in the house so early in the morning—and especially, one who stank.

"You heard her," *my friend* said. "Let's go get you cleaned up."

We walked through a couple of corridors, their stucco walls sparsely adorned, eventually reaching a small, roofed patio filled with the fragrance of blooming flowers.

"Alright," he said, showing me a wooden bathtub, "take off your clothes and jump in."

He didn't pay much attention to my nudity, although to be fair, it was only for an instant that I flashed my penis in front of him.

The water felt invigoratingly pleasant; a bath was exactly what I needed after all I had been through.

"Much better?" he asked after a while.

"Like I've been born again."

"You want me to scrub your back?" he asked, moving behind me.

"That would be wonderful."

I exposed my torso as he retrieved a sponge. Bliss enveloped me as he diligently scrubbed my shoulders and back.

"How long have you been out in the country?"

11

"Just yesterday."

"You look like you've been outside for months. It's a pity, since you're really pretty."

I quivered. *Did he just say I was pretty? What an odd thing for one boy to say to another.* But I liked it.

"Turn around."

He scrubbed my toned chest, which was nowhere near as strong as his. *Oh no! Maybe he wants to scrub my legs too.* My dick was already pointing outward; I had no way to hide it. This sometimes happened to me when I wrestled with other boys—I always took it as a natural body response to close body contact—but something felt different this time.

"Alright, I think we've managed to remove most of the dirt. You can dry off with a towel from over there," he said, pointing to a rack of sheepskins. "I'll go get you some new clothes."

The wool of the towels was the softest I had ever felt. Whoever these people were, they did not skimp on comfort. The simplicity of the place was somewhat deceptive.

"Here you go," he said, presenting me with a green tunic. "It's mine, but I've only worn it once or twice. It should fit you."

Fortunately my erection was gone and I wasn't embarrassed to have him see me naked again.

"It fits me perfectly," I said, putting it on.

"Try this too," he said, showing me a loincloth. "It's clean."

"Thank you." I was excited to wear something that had been on his private parts.

"Let's join my parents for *ientaculum*."

The robe carried a light, pleasant scent—his scent. I envisioned smelling that masculine aroma directly from his skin, but I compelled myself to turn away from such contemplations.

In the kitchen, Renatus's parents were already seated at a modest wooden table. His mother had switched to a stola designed for home wear, and her husband wore a well-worn, loose-fitting brown wool tunic that revealed a considerable portion of his hairy chest.

"Please come in and have a sit," she said as she took a bite of bread. "Eusebius, this is Renatus's new friend. His name is..."

"Lucius," I chimed in.

Eusebius—with a prominent, bulbous nose, plump lips, and a bald, egg-shaped head—looked nothing like Renatus, who apparently had inherited all his beauty from his mother. He wore a thick stubble, and his skin was deeply tanned, resembling a sailor back from the high seas.

"Lucius what?" he asked, arching his thick eyebrows, which had a few stray hairs.

"Modius," I made up.

"Modius... I've never heard of that family name, have you, Gaia?"

She shook her head.

"Are you from Pompeii?" He took a sip of milk. "As Renatus probably told you already, we're Pompeiians. We're just spending a little time in our villa."

13

"No, *domine*, I'm—" I began, about to tell another lie.

"Why are you asking so many questions?" Gaia intervened. "Can we just have a normal conversation?"

"We're meeting Renatus's friend for the first time, it's normal that I want to know more about him."

"He looks rather shy." Gaia looked into my eyes and smiled. "There's nothing to fear, my dear Lucius; you're among friends. Care for some bread and butter?"

As we ate, I observed my hosts more closely. Certainly, Eusebius might not qualify as a Greek statue model, but he had a very alluring masculine presence. Gaia was a lively woman, if maybe a bit too cheerful for her age. So unlike my mother.

The conversation became more casual as they talked about their love for their farm, the meticulous care they put into it, and the hard work required to run it, among other topics.

"You seem to have a good life here," I said, taking a sip. "That's all I wish for myself, a simple life with no complications."

"Did you hear that, Eusebius?" she said, hastening her bite of bread. "He might be a good candidate for the studies."

"Indeed." Eusebius rose to his feet and wiped his mouth with a cloth. "We shall see later; for now, I must retire to the *tablinum*. Make yourself at home, Lucius."

"That's my father, you know. A bookworm. And he wants me to become a philosopher."

"That's wonderful! You're lucky. My father wants me to practice law, like him."

"Your father..." Gaia said, making me regret bringing him into the conversation. "I still can't get my head around not knowing his family name. Your kin must come from far away. By the way, why were you wandering about in the woods? You're not a criminal, are you?"

"Mom!"

"I'm sorry. You don't seem that type anyway. In fact, I think I like you already." She smiled and stood up. "As my husband said, feel yourself at home. I'll be around, you know, doing *lady* things. Why don't you show him around the villa, Renatus?" She blew him a kiss and waved at me, squinting her eyes.

"Your parents are nice people," I said when she left.

"And wait until you know them a little better."

3

The following days went by in serenity. They didn't ask me to, but I willingly pitched in with picking, sorting, cleaning, and stomping grapes—this last activity being especially enjoyable. I also helped with putting the horses out to pasture, feeding the pigs, and gathering eggs for breakfast, among other tasks—there was no shortage of work. The slaves—whom Eusebius and Gaia treated very kindly—greeted me respectfully, akin to a cherished family member, and never engaged in conversation or—thank the gods—asked me questions. I spent most of my time with Renatus; sometimes he would read aloud excerpts from the philosophical texts his father made him study—a realm that eluded my comprehension. I enjoyed watching him recite; it offered me a good opportunity to listen to his voice while reveling in his gorgeous features.

Today, as dusk settled, he brought me to the barn. The sun's rays streamed serenely through the large windows, casting a golden glow on the neatly arranged haystacks. We concealed ourselves behind one of them as he signaled for me to be silent. After a brief moment, a tall, very muscular black man emerged. He was likely in his twenties, but it was hard to tell from a distance.

"Who is he?" I whispered.

"We call him Tullianus, but that's not his real name. He has never shared it with us."

"He's African, right?"

"Yes. From the Ethiopian steppes, as far as we know. He doesn't talk much."

"What does he do in the villa?"

"He's the foreman. He's really helpful to my father, you know."

"I can see why; he looks strong as a bull."

Tullianus removed his tunic, exposing his smooth and impressively sculpted ebony torso. As he untied his *subligaculum*, the sheer size of his member struck me.

"You've never seen anything like that before, right?"

"Not that I've seen many dicks in my life, but that one is like an elephant's trunk. I doubt any Roman man is endowed like that."

"I bet you're right. The men of this race are something else."

Tullianus lay comfortably on the straw, leaning against a haystack. He closed his eyes and caressed his chest and legs with his manly hands as the orange rays of the sunset tenderly kissed his sweaty skin.

"What is he doing?"

"Just watch," Renatus whispered with a smile. "He comes here every day when the sun goes down. I spy on him whenever I can."

As Tullianus continued to pleasure himself, his elephant cock stiffened, growing even larger. *By Priapus, even horses would be jealous of this amazing man.* He gently touched his balls, then moved to the shaft and up to the head, which he uncovered sliding down the prepuce, making his shiny, slick glans come to light. Trembling, I almost fell over, pulling one of the haystacks slightly out of place.

"Sorry," I hissed. "Do you think he found out we're watching him?"

"I don't think so. But even if he did, I doubt he would care." Renatus looked at me with sparkles in his eyes. "Do you want to try?"

"Try what?" I said, quivering.

He jerked his head. "Doing what he's doing."

"Ehm…" I was dying to, but didn't know if it was appropriate for me to admit it in front of my friend. What if he was just testing me?

"Come on… Don't tell me you've never done it."

"Of course I have, I mean… when I'm by myself."

"It's more exciting this way. I get off every time I come to see him. I wait to release my seed at the same time he does. It's hard though, because sometimes he lasts hours."

"Hours?"

"Joking. But he does take his time."

Renatus lifted his tunic and began to stroke his penis. I took a side glance, but he kept it covered with his *subligaculum*.

Mine had already begun to leak, so I lost my shyness and played along.

If Tullianus had turned around, he would have seen our drooling faces, but he never did. He seemed too self-absorbed to care about anything else.

He continued to tame his African snake, occasionally moistening his hand with spittle. After a while, his eyes squeezed shut and his mouth contorted into a grimace of pleasure. A white stream burst from his cock, landing two *cubiti* away from him on the straw, as he moaned and breathed heavily.

Renatus and I jerked off as fast as we could, struggling to hold back our moans as we orgasmed, our seed splattering the haystacks. Panting, we exchanged glances, sharing a mischievous smile. After hastily straightening our clothes, we hurried out of the barn, holding hands.

We spied on Tullianus a few more times over the next few days, sometimes jerking off to him, sometimes just watching him.

On this occasion, I stood next to my friend with my arm around his shoulders—our physical proximity being even more exciting than touching myself. We did not return home after our shenanigans; we waited for Tullianus to retire to his quarters before entering the barn, now sunk in a comfortable twilight.

Renatus invited me to recline beside him in the very spot where Tullianus had lain, the manly scent of the African and the sweet smell of his cum still permeating the air. So I did, and this time it was Renatus who put his left arm around my shoulders and laid his head on me. I instinctively put my right hand on his leg, over his robe. He pulled his clothes up, so that my hand could touch his bare skin. I shivered at the softness of the touch. I moved my hand slowly, caressing his leg and feeling his hairs rise. I moved my hand up a little more, until I reached his underwear. I stopped. My heart skipped a bit. *I've gone too far.*

I turned my head to look at him, but his eyes remained closed. When he opened them and smiled, I inadvertently expressed a plea with my face, silently seeking permission to touch him down there. He didn't nod or shake his head; he simply closed his eyes again. After an eternity, he loosened his *subligaculum*, so now I was certain I could move forward. I cautiously reached further up and felt that his manhood had grown hard. He took off his loincloth and moved slightly away from me to remove his tunic, which he placed under him as a sheet. Completely naked, lying next to me, he waited for me to continue what I was doing.

I quickly undressed and lay back down on his left side, placing my robe underneath, like him. I grabbed his fully erect cock and began to stroke it. Breathtaking beauty emerged in the contrast between my ivory hand and his richer, dusky skin. *I'm holding his dick—I'm really holding his dick!*

"Fuck," he whispered.

Wide-eyed, I kept jerking him off. He placed his leg over mine, which I caressed with my left hand. Now he moved his waist up and down, letting his cock slide inside my curled fingers. He looked at me, and rested his head on my shoulder once more, placing his hand behind my neck. I touched the tip of his cock, making a thread of precum between his cock hole and my index finger. I brought my right hand to my mouth and sucked my fingers, partly to get a taste of him and partly to provide more lubrication. Then I caressed his leg some more with my other hand. I masturbated him more vigorously, my breathing quickening with his. Squeezing his *membrum virile* brought out the giant mushroom-shaped head of the cock, and I cupped it, touching it and releasing it several times.

"Ahh, you bastard."

"Yes?" I asked, looking at him tenderly.

"Yes," he replied with bated breath, closing his eyes.

I touched his balls without taking my eyes off his face, which now showed a delirious expression. He bit his lips and moaned. I let go of his balls and slid my hand down his shaft, gripping his cock hard at the base and watching it stand like a rod of iron.

"When was the last time we cummed?" he whispered.

"Three days ago."

"It's going to be a full load then."

I varied my strokes, working at times on his head and at times on his shaft, feeling the tremors of his body with the erect hairs on my arm. I also took the opportunity to caress his beautiful chest, chiseled and strong, with some arousing hair in the cleft. The sparse hair in his armpit added to his charm, making him look both alluring and vulnerable in the position he was lying in.

"Go for it, come on." He pulled my hand to his neck.

I choked him slightly and increased the speed of the masturbation. His chest heaved as his breathing became heavier. I moved closer to him, my mouth desperately seeking his.

Our first kiss was nothing more than a timid touch. His full lips were a perfect match for mine, thin and delicate. When we parted, he grabbed my arm and looked at me, begging me not to stop. I responded to his gaze with the same expression of devotion. We kissed again, this time opening our mouths, feeling the rubbing of our tongues. Lightning flashed across my chest and stars danced in my belly.

He dared me to go harder, so I rubbed his cock with determination, as if milking a cow.

"Come on!" he said, slapping my arm.

I continued.

"Yes, fuck, yes, keep going, man!"

I stopped. "Please?"

"Please."

"Please?"

"Please!"

I resumed at full speed for a few more minutes, spitting on the head of his cock, watching my saliva enter his pee hole and mix with his precum. I also tapped his balls lightly.

"Ouch, asshole."

I chuckled and leaned over to lock lips with him again. Then I rested my elbow on his stomach and changed the angle of the masturbation to get a better grip of his hopelessly erect manhood, to which he responded by caressing my back and shoulders.

Then, I did the unthinkable: I took the slippery and salty head of his cock in my mouth. I had never dreamed of doing something like that, but it seemed the most natural thing to do.

"Oh man, make me cum now…"

I paused. "Please?"

"Yes! Don't stop, please, I'm so fucking close!"

I jerked him off harder.

"I'm going to cum now, man, I'm cumming!"

Two strong spurts came out of his cock followed by the rest of his seed descending on my fingers like hot lava. He moaned and groaned like a wounded beast.

"Ohh, *amice*, ohh!"

I put my hand over his mouth as I finished him off, smearing his cock and balls with his white syrup. He shook and yelped like a puppy.

As I took my hand away from his mouth, he grabbed me hard by the shoulders. "Fuck, fuck!"

I took pity on him and ended the delightful, post-orgasm torment, gazing at him with a smile. He closed his eyes, tilting his head back. I nestled on top of him, listening to the rhythm of his heartbeat. We lay there, our breathing as one, until we succumbed into blissful slumber.

4

That was of course not the only time. We jerked off several times a day in various places where we could not be seen. The day's chores became a blur; nothing held significance for me, except the moments when we delved into the sensations of our bodies. It bothered me that when we weren't doing it, Renatus acted as if there was nothing between us, leaving me uncertain whether our adventures would end as abruptly as they had begun.

I went to sweep the atrium to distract myself. What was this new feeling in my heart? I cared about Renatus, wanted to be near him all the time, I wanted to see him smile. Did he feel the same way? I remained still when I saw Gaia walking through the garden. His parents had to suspect something. *Don't be ridiculous, Lucius. There are no other boys our age around; it's only natural that we have developed a close bond with each other.* I returned to my task, procuring chatter from the slaves when they passed near me.

As the day ended, we returned to our *cubiculum*. We slept in bunk beds; our stay in the barn remained the only night we had cuddled up to sleep.

"Good night," I said to him with a kiss, before climbing into the top bunk.

I crawled under the blanket and fixed my gaze on the ceiling. Time drifted amid the chirping of crickets. Should I ask if I can sleep with him? I was about to speak, but I held back. So far I've preferred to let him take the lead, whether he invited me to jerk off or kiss. It felt more comfortable that way, and I didn't know what would happen if I changed the dynamics of our relationship.

Having managed only a few hours of sleep, I found myself tossing and turning in bed. Thirsty, I descended the ladder in search of water. With no amphora in the room, I had to venture outside. Carefully opening the door without a creak, I ensured that Renatus's light snoring remained undisturbed.

In the kitchen, I poured myself a goblet of water and gulped it down. A surge of curiosity pushed me to explore the house instead of returning to the *cubiculum*. I grappled with a sense of betraying my hosts' trust, but the desire to learn more about these people won me over.

The *tablinum* would likely hold the most clues. I had to find it. The moonlight filtering through the windows provided enough illumination to navigate the corridors. Guided by the typical placement of such rooms in a *domus*, I identified a door that seemed a probable candidate. With careful precision, I pushed it open, just enough for my slender frame to slip through. The musty aroma of papyri confirmed the accuracy of my choice. Unfortunately, the

25

room lacked windows, and without a candle, my visit wouldn't yield any results.

As I left the *tablinum*, a shiver told me that I was engaging in something very wrong. Rushing through the halls back to our room, I was startled by a muffled noise coming from somewhere in the house. Intrigued, I retraced my steps, looking for the source.

The sound became clearer as I reached a *cubiculum* door; it was a high-pitched human moan—coming from pleasure rather than pain. I peered through the crack. Renatus's parents were engaged in a physical, intimate activity that, although I knew existed, I had never witnessed before. She was lying on her back, legs spread wide on a large bed, and on top of her lay her husband, revealing the dark and hairy back and buttocks that gave him that wild boar-like appearance.

He moved rhythmically inside her as he kissed and sucked her breasts wildly amid deep grunts, to which she responded with moans and squeals. He rose and pinned her arms against the bed, pouncing on her even faster. A loud roar came out of his mouth, and he penetrated her a few more times before collapsing on the bed. I stood there mesmerized for a few moments at the sight of his sweaty chest, broad and hairy, as he lay with one arm across his forehead. A strange arousal coursed through me.

As I turned around to return to the bedroom, a pair of hands grabbed me and pressed me against the wall.

"What the hell are you doing here?" Renatus hissed.

Without giving me a chance to speak, he forcibly pulled me by the wrist.

"Please listen to me, I can explain."

"You'll do it in the bedroom."

He sat on the bed and gestured for me to sit beside him.

"I... was thirsty and went to get some water."

"You weren't coming back from the kitchen."

"I was, but—" *It should be alright if I leave out the part of the tablinum.* "I heard noises. I went to see where they came from. I thought your mother was crying or something."

"Do you expect me to believe that?"

"Of course! Why would I lie to you?" My heart cringed.

"Maybe you were trying to steal something."

I was hurt that he thought me capable of such a thing, but under the circumstances, it was a fair suspicion.

"Of course not, what do you take me for? Even if I stole something, where could I hide it?"

"You could run away. You seem pretty good at that."

Another blow. I felt so bad I wanted to cry. I wanted to hug him and kiss him and ask him to forgive me. I tried to do just that, but he pulled away.

"Don't tell me you've never seen what you saw in that room."

I shook my head.

"You've never spied on your parents?"

"No."

"But you had no scruples about spying on mine."

"I told you I wasn't trying. I heard the noises and I looked to see what it was. That's all."

A deep silence settled. My heart ached; his trust in me had been broken. I touched his arm. He didn't move.

"Renatus…"

"What?"

I shuddered at the question I was about to ask. "Do you…" I cleared my throat. "Do you think that… you and I… could do something like that?"

He looked at me with wild eyes. "Go to your bed now. It's almost dawn and we have hard work to do."

In the morning, Eusebius tasked us with preparing firewood. He led us to a pile of logs and provided us with a splitting maul. Renatus placed the first log on a tree stump and struck it with a precision that cleaved it neatly into two halves, which jumped vigorously to the sides. Then he split another. And another. It seemed as if he wanted to pour all his energy into the task, to take his mind off something that was troubling him. I asked if I could help, but he waved his hand dismissively.

"Pick up those pieces and stack them over there if you want to do something useful," he said after a while.

There was a certain annoyance in his voice that I had never sensed from him before, and it made me sad. I carried out my work quietly.

The whole morning went by, and he didn't speak to me again. We even ate lunch in silence. When evening came, I finally mustered the courage to do something I had been thinking about all day.

"Renatus."

"Yes."

"Would you like to… go to the barn?"

"No. I'm tired."

I should have let him invite me, as always. "What's wrong with you today?"

"I'm fine. Just leave me alone for a while, will you?"

It was the first time he had asked me to leave him alone. My heart sank. I turned away before my eyes betrayed my emotions.

I went alone to the barn and tried to pleasure myself—if only to take my mind off things—but it just didn't work. Even the memories of our many past experiences failed to arouse me.

A strong wind was blowing through the windows, and I felt cold. I wished he was there holding me, comforting me. I hugged myself and slowly fell asleep.

As I woke up, darkness had already descended, bringing with it an even colder chill in the air. I returned to the house, uncertain if he would allow me to sleep in his room. He was lying on his bed, clutching a wineskin.

"Have you been drinking?"

He remained silent.

"Why?"

He shrugged, a forlorn expression on his face.

I lay down beside him. "It's what I said last night, isn't it? I'm sorry; I was stupid to even ask something like that. Please forgive me, I beg you."

He extended the wineskin to me. I took a large gulp. The liquid raced down my throat so fast I almost choked.

"Easy, the night is long."

I was very glad to hear him speak in a more cheerful tone. I put my arm around him and leaned my head on his shoulder.

"It's good wine. My father saves it for special occasions."

I remained silent for a long while. "Is this a special occasion?"

He gazed at me sweetly and we merged into a blissful kiss, immediately dispelling all the tension between us. He nimbly removed my clothes, and I did the same with his. His caresses on my back and buttocks showed an urge he had never shown before, making my dick spring. Anxiously, he went kissing down my neck and pecs, sucked my nipples and returned to my mouth. Both of our cocks had begun to leak, so I grabbed his and rubbed it against mine, feeling its comforting warmth. I went down on him with all the passion that had surged in me since the night before, when I imagined him doing to me the things Eusebius did to his wife. He moaned in pleasure, pushing my head down, making sure to keep his cock touching my throat. He released me only when I gagged, but I immediately went back to avidly sucking my favorite part of his.

"Get on all fours," he said, patting me on the shoulder. "I want to do something different tonight."

He pulled my asscheeks apart and a wet tingle in my anus made me quiver. He spat on my most intimate part and licked it again, lightly inserting his tongue into it; it felt like the touch of an eel. Standing on the side of the bed, he slapped his wet cock against my ass cheeks, then rubbed it in the crack.

"Do you really want to know what it's like to have a man inside you?"

"Yes." *It's all I want in the world.*

"Let me know if it hurts."

"Ow," I uttered when I felt the first pressure of the head entering me.

"Should I back out?"

"No, no, just let me get used to it."

He paused for a few moments, then pushed a little more.

"Ahh, slow please!"

He thrusted as gently as possible, and a hard-to-explain feeling of fullness invaded my rear. He was balls deep inside me now, his pubic hair tickling me. I panted as my hole throbbed beyond my control.

"Easy, man. Do you want me to take it out?"

"Yes, but slowly."

I felt the recoil with relief. Soon he pushed himself in again, this time more easily.

"Ahh! By all the gods, this feels so good."

"And we're just getting started."

He took another gulp of wine and passed me the skin. Moving a little faster, he sent a surge of pleasure coursing through me like lightning. I felt as if I were undergoing a medical procedure and carried transported to Olympus in Apollo's chariot at the same time. He grabbed my hips for support and fucked me harder, making me squeal like a piglet. He stopped and tapped my buttocks to make me lie on my back.

"That's better. Now I can see your delirious face when I'm inside you."

Bathed in the soft glow of candlelight, his exquisite face glistened amid copious beads of sweat. He entered me again, this time in one stroke. My asshole had become numb to the pain and welcomed only pleasure. I wanted him to never take his cock out of me. He put his hands on my pecs and fucked me harder. I leaned my head back and half closed my eyes.

"That's what I mean," he said as he punished my hole with all his might. "I'm going to cum now! Ohh!"

I felt a gush of liquid pour inside me as his penetrations became less frequent, but more forceful.

"Yes! Take it all inside! Ohh!" He collapsed on the bed, breathing heavily. "Now, it's your turn," he said a few moments later, rising and turning to me. He inserted two fingers in my sloppy hole as he energetically masturbated me.

I had already been on the verge of exploding when he was inside. "I'm going to cum now! Ahh!"

My milk spurted out in a hot stream, hitting him in the face. When I was done, he looked at me, licking my jism from his lips. Then he gave me the most incredible kiss, sweetened with the taste of my cum.

The morning chill found us cuddling. I woke up when I felt him reaching for a blanket.

"Renatus," I whispered to his ear. "We must go bathe now." The smell of sex was so strong that anyone would recognized it immediately.

He jumped out of bed.

We went to the bath and took a dip with a splash. Renatus started a water fight, and I eagerly reciprocated. In the middle of our game, Eusebius appeared.

"There you are! I figured you'd be exhausted from splitting firewood yesterday. Today you overslept."

"That was nothing, Dad. We can split twice as much, right, Lucius?"

If you let me help, yeah.

Eusebius then did something that struck me as odd. He took off his clothes quite naturally and joined us in the pool. Glancing at him, I confirmed that his body resembled that of a boar: big, fat, and extremely hairy all over. *Renatus doesn't have that look at all.* Another thing that caught my attention was his phallus. It was like a shrunken version of himself, shriveled and buried inside a dense bush.

Something about Eusebius unsettled me. He exuded a profound sexuality, like no other man I had ever met before. Or maybe I was noticing it now because having sex with Renatus had awakened me to a new world of pleasure.

Eusebius emerged from the water and wiped his face. "Do you want to have breakfast? Gaia can make us some wonderful quail eggs."

5

"I'm listening to what you're saying but nothing sticks in my head."

"Let's try this one more time. I'm going to read it again slowly, but don't let your mind wander away, alright?"

We were lying on the straw in the barn—where we had so many times pleasured ourselves—but this time, Renatus wanted to treat me to a different experience: an "intellectual journey," as he put it. I wasn't naturally inclined toward deep thinking, but any opportunity to lie beside him was more than welcome. He had brought scrolls from his father's library and was reading me passages he deemed not too dense for my understanding.

"What was the name of that philosopher again?" I stifled a yawn.

"Epicurus. The wisest man who ever lived."

"Never heard of him."

"He isn't taught by any tutor in Rome. My father knows of him because he came from Greece. He brought along many manuscripts and translated them into Latin himself."

"That must have been a lot of work."

"It was." He rose to his feet. "Hence, you must pay attention."

I tried to concentrate on his oratory, but after a while I found myself lost again in the exquisite sight of his features.

"So what do you think?" he asked, abruptly snapping me out of my fantasies.

"Can you just explain to me what's being said? I'm struggling to digest all the jargon."

"Alright," he said, rolling his eyes. "This book is called *De rerum natura* and was written not by the master himself, but by one of his disciples in later centuries, the Roman poet Lucretius."

"Uh-huh."

"The first volume discusses the gods and how they do not interfere in human life."

"Wait a minute. Are you saying our lives aren't determined by the will of the gods and their wrath or benevolence?"

"That's right. Life's events are shaped by our own actions and acts of chance. The universe moves on its own, not according to the will of any god, but following its own laws."

"But how can there be laws without a legislator."

"It's a figure of speech. By laws I mean things that occur on a regular basis, but which are by no means eternal or immutable: change is the only permanent thing in existence."

I looked at him with a furrowed brow.

"All the things around us," he continued, pacing around, "both inert and living are composed of tiny little things called atoms, which are in a perpetual state of motion and combine based on their properties, which means—"

"Hold on," I said, standing in front of him. "What you're saying doesn't make sense. How can you compare a plant or an animal to a rock? Obviously, they're not made of the same thing."

"Once the life force leaves those beings, they are. It doesn't take long for them to return to the earth they are made of."

"And what is this life force, where does it go after death?"

"It's the soul. But unlike what you might think, it doesn't exist outside of the body; once the body dies, it dissipates into the universe."

"Then, what happens to us after we die?"

"Nothing. We simply cease to exist."

"Surely you can't believe that." Now it was me pacing around. "There must be something, some kind of afterlife, a reward for the heroes and a punishment for the wicked."

"There's no such thing. But the good part is, you should not fear death. When we're here, death is not, and when death is here, we're not. Death is nothing to us."

Death is nothing to us. I had never entertained such a powerful thought. This philosophy was starting to interest me.

In the days that followed, we carried on with our activities as usual, that is, amid fucking and mutual masturbation. At some point I should have grown weary of it all, but on the contrary, my desire kept increasing. I was living an experience that I didn't want to end, and I had more stamina for everything, including work.

This morning, Eusebius had joined us in our outdoors activities, wearing an oversized brown tunic with the collar ripped into a V-shape, cinched loosely with a belt. The glorious sight of his hairy chest was agonizingly arousing; it possessed a divine force of attraction that drew me to him. I found myself yearning to feel his arms around me and bask in his warmth. *But he's the father of Renatus—my partner, the man I love!*

Granting us a respite from our work, Eusebius headed back to the house. We stayed outside, leaning against a tree, making use of the time to enjoy some fruit.

"So, before me, you'd never been with a man, am I right?" Renatus asked, biting an apple.

The question almost made me choke. "Of course not. You should have noticed it when you first entered me."

"I did, you were very tight," he said with a cynical grin.

"Then, why did you ask?"

"I thought maybe you could have taken the active role with a slave or a cousin."

"No. I had never had sex with anyone before."

"Not even with a woman?"

"I could never have sex with a woman. I have too much respect for them to do something that might hurt them. Besides, I'm not attracted to them." *Why do I have to give him this pointless explanation now?* "Are you?"

"I thought I was, until I met you."

"So have you…?"

"Only a few times, with two of my mom's maids. Naughty old bitches. I didn't care for them at all, but they taught me a few tricks. It was just my opportunity to, you know, stick my dick into something."

"But haven't you thought about marriage?"

"Not really. My parents don't care for it. They believe it's better for philosophers not to marry."

"I see their point."

"Alright," he said, getting up, "let's now delve into our studies."

"I have an idea for something more entertaining," I said in a silly tone, getting up as well.

"You smutty boy," he said, pulling me down to the grass, where we tumbled together. "This time I'm going to fulfill your desires, but afterward, we must study!"

We made love three, four, five times that day. At some point I lost count.

At night, I was in the kitchen looking for snacks to bring to the bedroom, when I heard again the mischievous noises that had gotten me in trouble with Renatus. I couldn't resist the curiosity to see Eusebius in action again, so I headed for their *cubiculum*.

The scene I saw through the crack horrified me. This time it was not Eusebius fucking Gaia, but Tullianus. Her intense high-pitched moans were not surprising given the colossal size of the African man's member. I could not believe how she had had the audacity to cheat on her husband in their own bedroom. But what I saw next shocked me even more: Eusebius was actually in the room, standing next to the bed, stroking his hard cock. My heart leaped into my throat. *Who are these people?*

Eusebius looked in my direction. Uncertain if he had noticed me, I hurried back to our room, swiftly shutting the door. Leaning against it, my breathing came in agitated gasps.

"What happened, why are you shaking?"

"Nothing." I handed Renatus the cheese, bread, and honey.

"Let me guess, you heard noises in my parents' bedroom again," he quipped with a chuckle.

"Yes…"

"When will you stop spying on them, you pig? We can do much better things together here."

If he only knew what his parents were actually up to.

I put a small piece of bread and honey in his mouth and gave him a peck on the cheek. We ate in silence, but after a few minutes we went back to kissing and touching. By now we had become one; there wasn't a single part of his body that I hadn't touched, kissed, or licked.

I was still quivering from all the love we had made that day; my muscles felt soft and my skin, warm and tender.

"I don't know if I still have any cum in me."

"It doesn't matter," he said, kissing my neck. "It's still delightful when the cock spasms without sperm."

He put me on all fours on the floor. Soon, his iron rod was penetrating me once more, my hole by now expecting the upcoming pressure. He was riding me hard while pulling my hair back, when the door opened, and there we were, naked, defenseless, and interlocked in front of Eusebius. *What will become of me now? Eusebius will beat me and throw me out of the house like the whore I am.* And Renatus? What would he do to him? Kill him?

Eusebius approached us with a composed gait, closing the door behind him. He stood still for a few moments.

"Can you step aside, Son?"

Renatus got off me and I remained in the same position, trembling. Eusebius came closer and I could sense the full force of his masculine aura taking possession of me, claiming me as his own. I wanted to say no, to beg him to leave, but my body was burning with unquenchable desire; I wanted him inside. I turned my head to meet his gaze, as he waited for my answer to the unspoken question.

After glancing briefly at Renatus, I turned my head back to Eusebius and, with a pleading gesture, gave him the permission he sought. The man of the house positioned himself behind me. In no time he was entering me; his sausage felt at least twice as thick as Renatus's. He rode me, thrusting again and again, slapping my ass and spitting copiously on my hole, causing me a torrent of pleasure that merged with the residual sensations I still had left from all the sex with Renatus that day.

"That's what you wanted, right, boy?" he said in a gruff voice. "You wanted me since the first time you saw me, didn't you? Now you got your old man too."

The teasing that came out of his mouth excited me even more. I could hardly believe the intensity of the experience I was living. After a few moments, Eusebius cummed inside me amid loud grunts. After his jism flooded my guts, he dropped onto the bed.

"Come here, boy, come here to daddy."

Renatus remained there just watching.

I lay down on his chest, giving myself the opportunity to stroke his glorious hair. My skin had become hypersensitive; every part of my body responded with sparkling intensity.

"You feel safe now, boy?" He hugged me tightly.

In that moment, I did feel very safe and comfortable, as if I could lose myself sleeping on his chest.

"You still haven't cummed yet. Cum for me now, boy. Cum for daddy."

I jerked off as hard as I could, until the few drops I had left came out and with them, the rest of my vitality. My whole body spasmed several times. Eusebius wiped off the jism off my dwindling prick with his hand and put it in his mouth. Then, he tongue-kissed me, as he wrapped me in his body, our sweaty smells mingling in a heady fragrance.

"Good boy," he said, tapping my shoulder. He rose and smoothed his tunic. "Now I must go back to my wife." *As if he owed me an explanation.*

After Eusebius left the room, a sudden chill swept over me. Renatus lay down beside me, offering his warmth, but something felt wrong, very wrong. I got up and climbed the ladder to hide in my bed.

6

I couldn't sleep that night. The wooden beams of the ceiling seemed to bear down on me, oppressing me with their weight. The moonlight filtering through the windows cast unsettling shadows on the walls, and the distant chirping of crickets outside only exacerbated my anxiety.

An unendurable force pulsed through my anus, a stark reminder of the momentary lapse that had ruptured the tranquility of the love between Renatus and me. I felt dirty, ashamed. Inside my head, a cacophony of voices—the haunting whispers of spirits from hell—pushed me to the edge of insanity. I covered my ears in a desperate attempt to silence them.

When did the attraction for Eusebius first stir within me? Undeniably, it went back to the first *ientaculum. What a hungry bitch have I been all this time.* And for how long had he known? He must have noticed my attention when we bathed together, reading the unspoken language of desire that I thought I had concealed—the subtle glances, the stolen moments of connection. What about Renatus? Had he also known all along? He didn't seem too shocked when his father entered the room.

Now he was sleeping soundly in the bunk bed below me, his rhythmic breathing a clear testimony of his nonchalance, but for me the air was unbreathable. Weeks had gone by in perfection, but now the lines of our love had become blurred, and it was all my fault. But maybe it was his fault too. Why didn't he stop me? Why didn't he—I tugged at my hair in despair.

At dawn, I walked through the austere corridors of the villa, the cool marble beneath my feet contrasting sharply with the burning turmoil within me. I found Renatus in the kitchen amid the aroma of freshly baked bread. The warmth that once filled his eyes now gave way to a distant, brooding gaze.

I sat beside him, watching him as he slathered butter onto a slice of bread. My stomach churned with anxiety. I wanted to speak, but the words wouldn't come out.

After finishing his meal, he got up and left me alone in an oppressive silence.

The morning passed in an uneasy dance of avoidance. As Renatus focused on his duties around the villa, I visited the olive pressing room, in an attempt to distract myself from the thoughts that tortured my mind. Felix, a slave, was working at one of the sturdy wooden structures with a large grinding stone.

"Good morning. Could you explain to me how the press works?"

He looked at me slightly startled. "Of course, young master, Lucius." He stopped his work. "First, we gather the ripe olives from the trees," he said, pointing at the baskets brimming with plump, purple olives, "then we clean and sort them, removing leaves and branches. Afterward we place the olives on this platform." Felix demonstrated the process, spreading a layer of olives on the concave stone. "Now comes the grinding. We must walk in circles, rolling this wheel over the olives, crushing them into a coarse paste."

And I thought my work was heavy.

"Finally we place the crushed olive paste in these mats and stack them on top of each other. This stack is what we place in the press under the center of this beam, which is attached to the wall on that end. Then we gradually add stones to the other end to apply pressure to the olives, squeezing out the oil, which is collected underneath in these baskets. Do you want to try it?"

I added the stones as he had instructed, and observed the oil run to the pots.

"Do you still have to clean the oil?"

"Not really, we just wait for it to float to the top, as it separates from water naturally, and then we store it in these amphorae."

I spent the whole afternoon in the olive pressing room and at sunset I went for a walk in the countryside to let the gentle wind finish clearing my mind. I spotted Renatus in the distance, the fading sunlight casting a golden glow on his features. He was throwing nuts at squirrels, watching them scurry to retrieve their prizes. A blissful scene of peace and simplicity, reminding me of the true nature of the man I had fallen for. *If we could only talk about what happened...*

As night fell, we stood in the courtyard, but neither he nor I did anything to lessen the awkwardness that beset us. He left before I could muster the courage to start a conversation, and I stayed outside for a while. His demeanor made me feel irritated. Didn't he feel the same way I did? Why didn't he seem to care about what happened? Why didn't he take the first step to talk about it, as he did with everything else?

When I entered our room, he was lying on his bed, as if waiting for me to join. But I still couldn't do it. Eusebius's touch lingered on my skin; I couldn't let Renatus hold me while I felt this way. Having sex was the furthest thing from a solution.

So we went to sleep again, after the coldest day in our relationship, if what we had could be called a "relationship." His silence felt like a wall falling over me. I made a decision: regardless of the consequences, I wasn't going to let this situation continue for another day.

The following morning, Renatus got up while I was still in bed. He saw me descend the ladder as he slipped on his sandals, his eyes meeting mine, void of any greeting. Just as he was leaving the room, I leaped between him and the door.

"What's wrong with you?" he said, irritation evident in his expression.

"What's wrong with you, I say. Why didn't you say a word to me all day yesterday?"

"You didn't say a word either."

"After what happened the night before? After you let your father fuck me in front of you?"

"Wasn't that what you wanted? You made no attempt to stop him."

"True, but you shouldn't have allowed it."

He chuckled. "Why should I deny you of your pleasure?"

"Because I'm your… because we're…"

"Friends, that's what we are."

I stood there, speechless, witnessing the beautiful connection we had nurtured crumble into a simple "friendship." I had resolved the night before that I would take responsibility for my actions, but the fact that he seemed so uncooperative made me want to attribute all the blame to him.

I hastily put on my sandals and stormed out of the room into the open field, attempting to vanish into the woods I had come from.

"Wait!" He chased after me.

I came to a halt but refrained from facing him. He caught me and enfolded me from behind.

"Why are you doing this?" he said to my ear. "We're friends."

"Friends?" I asked, breaking away and turning to him. "After all those days and nights we've shared? What we do is not what friends do, *domine*."

"You can't be my wife. You're not a woman."

"No, but I can be—"

"My husband? That doesn't exist. Not in Rome."

I stood still, my eyes open for the first time to the fragility of my position. Here I was, a young adult, surrendering my body and my honor to another male, oblivious to the fact that a wider world awaited, where one day I would be held accountable. He took me in his arms again and, this time, all my defenses crumbled.

"It's alright," he said, caressing the back of my head. "Not everything needs to be drama. Now you know why I was hesitant to make love to you. I desired you from the start, but I knew this could happen. Sex is great but can lead to anxiety and despair if you don't know how to handle it. That's why we need the philosophy."

"But what happened with your father..." I said, pulling away from him.

"He's not my father," he said, locking eyes with me. "He married my mom when she became pregnant, and the man refused to marry her. Eusebius saved her from a life of disgrace."

"But... does he love her?" I tried to make sense of what I had witnessed in their bedroom.

"Of course. They know each other from the studies of the philosophy. Epicureanism doesn't differentiate between men and women... at least not in matters of intellect. Women have the same right as men to study it. It made a lot of sense for them to build a life together."

"Then why didn't they have children of their own."

"They already had me and didn't want to burden themselves with a larger family. Besides, she's well aware of Eusebius's inclinations, but he doesn't deprive her of her pleasure either. Pleasure is their sole pursuit. That's why you saw what you saw."

I gaped. "So, you knew that they bring Tullianus into their bedroom?"

He nodded. "And they both knew about us too. Don't think they're stupid. They're totally alright with it."

I couldn't fathom what I was hearing. What was this bizarre world I had gotten myself into?

"Eusebius told me that he had sensed that you were attracted to him. He asked me if I thought you would like him to fuck you. I told him that I didn't know and that he should ask you. And then it happened."

"But didn't you feel jealous?"

He laughed. "Why should I feel jealous? We're friends, with benefits, of course. The day you understand the true meaning of friendship, you'll feel the same way I do."

"No, I don't understand, I don't understand it at all! I love you, Renatus, can't you see? What happened with your father was... I don't even know what it was, just an overpowering force that drew me in. But no more than that, I swear!"

"You owe me no explanation, Lucius. Always remember... pleasure... pleasure is the only thing that matters in this world. You shouldn't deny yourself of it."

I shook my head in disbelief, no longer willing to listen. I ran back to the house, where Eusebius was waiting at the door.

"Don't you dare touch me, you pig! You're sick, both of you are!"

As I ran inside the villa I overheard Gaia say to Eusebius: "He's not quite ready for the philosophy yet."

Instead of heading to Renatus's bedroom, I retreated to the one they had provided me with when I first arrived. I slipped beneath the blankets, curling up into a ball. I didn't light any candles or open the curtains; I just lay there in darkness, trapped in the obscurity of my thoughts. Would they cast me out of the house now? I felt fear, but also repulsion; I felt used as a vessel for their pleasure. These men, who had been so familiar to me, had now become strangers again. I was disgusted with myself, my body and what I had become.

After lying in bed for hours, a loud noise startled me. I got up and cautiously cracked the door open. The unmistakable sound of heavy banging echoed from the front door. I ventured out of my room, crossed the small backyard garden, and positioned myself behind a pillar. The family rushed out into the *vestibulum*.

"*Salve, domine*," a man said. "We are in search of a young man who has been missing for several days. Have you noticed anyone wandering around your villa recently?"

"No. Have you, Renatus?"

"No, Dad."

"It is of utmost importance that you inform us promptly if you encounter anyone matching this description." The man extended a small papyrus scroll to Eusebius. "A substantial reward awaits you if you assist us in locating him." He paused. "On the other hand, if you hide him…"

"Why would we do that?" Eusebius replied.

"The notice includes an address in Neapolis where you can report any information. Have a good day."

Eusebius gave Gaia the scroll without unrolling it. He and Renatus withdrew from the door, and I hastened back to my room before they caught sight of me. I burrowed under the covers, my only sanctuary. Moments later, there was a soft knock on the door. I didn't answer. Slowly, the door creaked open. Eusebius approached my bed, while Renatus drew back the curtains, allowing light to infiltrate the room.

"Who are you, Lucius Modius?" Eusebius asked.

Despite the room's chill, beads of sweat formed on my skin. "If you don't want me here, I'd be better off leaving," I said, jumping out of bed and making a dash for the door.

Renatus grabbed my arm. "Where are you going? There are armed men looking for you."

"What are you hiding from, Lucius?" Eusebius asked. "You'd better speak up now."

"I won't say a word. Now if you'll just let me go, please? You're hurting me."

Renatus released his grip.

I sat on a chair, tugging at my hair. *I can't say anything. I won't say anything. They must never know why I escaped. They wouldn't understand.* "You can't force me to speak."

"We won't force you, Lucius," Renatus said. "But you have to trust us. How can we protect you if we don't know what you're up against?"

"My name is Lucius, I never lied about that." I sighed. "We're dealing with someone very dangerous who's threatening my life. I knew he would come after me. I just can't escape him."

"Escape whom?" Renatus asked, pulling another chair close to mine and wrapping his arm around my shoulders.

"I think it's best for all of us to go to Pompeii," Eusebius said. "It's not safe for Lucius to stay here."

I looked at both of them, startled.

"Yes," Renatus said. "Let's go to Pompeii. It will do you good."

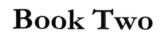

Book Two

7

I remained silent along the way. Even the clear blue sky and the warm rays of the morning sun could not brighten my mood. The gentle trot of the horses guided our carriage through dozens of farms and opulent villas, occasionally stumbling upon a few misplaced stones on the lengthy and well-maintained *via Romana*. I spent most of my time gazing out the window. Endless acres of green filled my eyes, and though the crisp mountain air was a delight to breathe, it failed to dispel the persistent turmoil in my mind. My adoptive family wasn't talking either. I wasn't sure if it was out of consideration for my unease or if they simply had nothing to say to each other. Back in the distance loomed Mount Vesuvius, ominous as ever. I had yet to fully shake off the memory of standing atop it, when it felt as if it would swallow me alive.

The road curved sharply downhill and continued along the shoreline. Dozens of fireclay tiled roofs overlooked the bay, sprawled across the rugged hills over a series of white and yellow terraces, their flowerbeds slumbering peacefully beneath the shade of colossal umbrella pines.

The port came into view, bustling with men unloading crates of imports and exports. To the left, about a quarter mile from the sea, were the outer walls of Pompeii. Tall, though not as imposing as those in Neapolis, their construction materials indicated that they had been built at various times by different peoples. As we approached the entrance, which I was informed was called the "Herculaneum gate," the sentries requested the family documents, which Eusebius produced, and had no problem explaining that I "was a friend of his son, visiting from Neapolis." The guards let us in with no further questions. It was evident that he's a well-respected man; his word held more weight than a simple papyrus.

Once inside the city, we passed by several houses, reminiscent in size and elegance of those in the finest neighborhoods of Neapolis. Luxury pervaded every corner; no doubt the reason why affluent Neapolitans—and Romans in general—favored spending their holidays here.

A few blocks further, the city became livelier as more people walked the streets, busy going about their daily routines, pulling carts, carrying jugs, conversing with one another. The pungent smell of fish and meat coming from the *macellum* signified our arrival to the city center. The forum, grand and magnificent, was abuzz with people engaged in the buying and selling of clothes, pottery, and a multitude of commodities. Temples dedicated to Jupiter, Apollo, and Venus graced the surroundings.

Our path continued through the *decumanus maximus*. Along this main thoroughfare there were several inns offering local delicacies and wines, spa centers providing massage services, at least two bathing facilities, numerous bakeries, and small shops located in front of people's dwellings. Many other buildings lined the streets, their purposes unknown to me.

Eusebius's *domus* was located at the end of a block. Its unassuming façade—painted in white with red dados and with a commonplace terracotta roof—accurately reflected the modesty of the interior. The walls of the atrium were covered with simple but beautiful frescoes depicting scenes from everyday life in Pompeii. Colorful mosaics with intricate patterns graced the floor surrounding the *impluvium*, and various potted plants and flowers in the corners added a touch of natural beauty.

A group of slaves welcomed us with reverence and warm smiles. Eusebius informed them that I was a guest and ordered them to treat me as a member of the family. Renatus promptly invited me to accompany him on a tour of the house. It featured a pleasant peristyle garden, enclosed by columns and a shaded roofed portico, whose interior walls were adorned with wall paintings depicting idyllic scenes of leisure in the countryside. At the center, a small fountain was surrounded by a coquettish little garden, its gentle flowing water creating a soothing ambiance. There was a complete absence of *lares* or statues of gods, something highly unusual for a Roman *domus*. However, after the conversation I had had with Renatus, it made perfect sense. If they did not believe in the will of the gods, it was logical that they saw no reason to pay homage to them.

Toward the rear of the house were the living quarters of the domestic slaves. These accommodations were far from shabby, in fact, they looked more comfortable than the modest *insulae* where the majority of the Roman free population of Neapolis resided. There was also a spacious bath with a *hypocaustum* for the private use of the family, connected to the city water supply.

Finally, Renatus took me to my room. I felt a twinge of sadness that we wouldn't sleep together anymore, but somehow I also felt relieved. Things were now undeniably different. A distant, yet cordial atmosphere had settled between us, like that among relatives who are not particularly close. I wanted to believe he was merely giving me space, but maybe things would never go back to what they were. I was trapped between my past and a new reality I didn't understand.

Shortly after Renatus left me alone, fatigue overcame me, and I drifted into slumber. When I woke up, a slave brought me fresh clothes and said I could use the bath if I so desired. I did. Back in the room, the same slave informed me that the family awaited me for *prandium* in one of the small *triclinii*. I joined them, and an awkward silence took place again. I made no attempt to dispel it. After finishing my meal, I quietly excused myself and retreated to my room, leaving them the space to converse privately, away from my presence.

I was dying to hold Renatus in my arms; I missed the taste of his kisses so much. Yet the memory of that night with him and his "father" continued to haunt me like a relentless specter.

Late in the afternoon I heard a gentle knock on the door. I said to come in. It was Gaia. She sat on the bed beside me.

"Lucius, I was planning on taking a stroll around town and maybe do some shopping, would you care to join me?"

"Is everyone going?"

"No. Just you and me."

Despite my despondency, the idea sounded appealing. I hadn't really spent much time with Gaia since this whole adventure began and the thought of being in her company, just the two of us, offered a sense of solace.

"Sure. Let me get ready."

After changing my robe and tidying my hair, I met her in the garden. As soon as she saw me, she took the keys and asked a slave to oversee the house during our absence.

"Where did Eusebius and Renatus go?" I asked as we walked along the cobblestone sidewalks of the street adjacent to the house.

"They had business to attend to."

If she was a mean person she would have responded something like, "What do you care?" but her kindness shone through in her response.

We reached the busiest streets, where musicians were playing for a coin, children running around, and people strolling amid friendly chatter.

"Would you like a honeyed ice?"

"Yes," I said with a smile.

"Two to go, please," she told the vendor.

The man opened a large copper pot that he kept in the shade, from which he scooped two balls of ice. He placed each one atop sweet bread adorned with dried fruits and nuts, which he drizzled with honey and sprinkled with sesame seeds.

"It's better than what we have in Neapolis."

"Neapolis… It's been a long time since we've been there."

Gaia's company made me feel safe, but deep inside, I still grappled with remorse and shame. Did she know I had fucked her husband? If she did, how could she not hate me for it? I still found it hard to believe what Renatus had told me. I didn't want to bring it up, it was too disturbing a topic for such a beautiful day. If the reason she had taken me out was to talk about it, I was prepared to come forward and apologize.

She told me about other people who lived on the same street as them, like Julius Polybus and Julia Felix, whom she described as a "very wealthy bitch." We approached the intersection with the *cardo maximus*, where the Temple of Isis stood.

"Do you ever pray in temples, Gaia?"

She chuckled. "Certainly not in this one, honey. It's for Egyptian immigrants. But no, I don't attend services at any of the other temples either."

"Why not?"

"I thought Renatus had discussed this with you. It's futile to pray to the gods, any of them. If they exist, they are indifferent to our concerns, but I'm more inclined to believe they don't exist at all."

I let out a gasp.

"Don't take it to heart, dear Lucius," she said with a smile. "Nothing in life is to be taken seriously. We're here only for a short time, and then we're gone forever; we might as well enjoy ourselves while we can."

She ran into an acquaintance, with whom she struck up a conversation. I took advantage of the moment to observe my surroundings. The street was lined with upscale shops, showcasing luxurious clothing and accessories from the Orient: expensive silks, gold bracelets, and Egyptian hematite amulets. Two theaters and the barracks and *palaestra*, where gladiators were training, were located behind the Temple of Isis. I felt bad for those men. All that effort just to entertain illiterate mobs. I had always found such spectacles repugnant. I could never comprehend how Romans could derive pleasure from the suffering of both humans and animals. Some of those males were worth looking at, though. If I ever attended a gladiator show, it would only be to witness their bulky muscles in action.

A group of men were queuing up at the entrance to a bathhouse located a few steps away from where I left Gaia. I approached and sneaked a peek inside, but the doorkeeper shooed me away like a stray cat. I went around the corner and came across another building, painted in bright colors, where provocatively dressed women were loitering outside. One of them came up to me. "Come on, honey. Would you like me to show you a good time?" I bolted back to rejoin Gaia.

"I'm sorry I got tangled up in a conversation. But I see you've taken the opportunity to see more of the city. How do you like it so far?"

"Everything looks really fancy. There's a lot of money here, right?"

"Yes. Many aristocratic families live in Pompeii. They take pride in their city. Most of the monuments are very well maintained. The only ones still in ruins are those damaged by the earthquake years ago. The city council hasn't yet decided whether to restore them or build them again. Many date back to the time of Augustus, so they hold both sentimental and historical value." She paused. "We get a lot of tourism too. People visit from all corners of Italy, and even as far as Greece and Egypt. The local merchants certainly know how to take their money, so they too enjoy prosperity."

"What about crime? Some people don't have appreciation for public buildings," I said, pointing to the graffiti on the theaters' walls.

"Well, that happens in every city. Pompeii is no exception, but it is kept much more under control here. You don't run into trouble, unless you actively seek it out."

I nodded.

"There is a much larger amphitheater behind our house. I'll show it to you another day. We might even attend a play by one of the Greek theater companies that come to the city from time to time."

"Do they perform in Latin, or Greek? I'm afraid my Greek is very rudimentary... it goes back to my childhood, and I've never really worked on it."

"They speak Latin, with a heavy accent, but you can understand it. It'll be fun." As we made our way back home, she added, "You spotted the baths, right?"

"Yeah. The man at the door didn't want to let me peek without paying."

"That's the norm," she said with a smile. "You should join us next time. I like to go there with Eusebius and Renatus every once in a while."

The mention of their names made me shudder. The couple of hours spent outside had momentarily put them out of my mind, but now they were back.

"Why do you go to public baths when you have such splendid ones at home?"

"Public baths serve not only for bathing but also for socializing. It's much more refreshing, if you'll pardon the pun, to meet your acquaintances there than in the formal setting of a *domus*. You really have to experience it for yourself. I'm sure you'll enjoy it."

8

A few days later, as Gaia had suggested, we gathered to visit the baths located at the intersection of Pompeii's two primary thoroughfares. Although I was relieved that we were segregated by gender at the entrance—I had no desire to see pussy—at the same time a pang of apprehension struck me when Gaia vanished beyond the door, and I was left alone with the only two men in the world who had taken me.

Eusebius paid the entrance fee, and we proceeded through a tunnel, the air becoming increasingly humid. We disrobed in the *apodyterium*, leaving our garments on designated racks that were watched by guards. We kept only our sandals and wrapped a towel around our waists. The walls of the room featured paintings of nude men flexing their brawny arms, making excitement grow under my towel. Affluent old men with refined manners were accompanied by slave boys carrying their bathing essentials: sheepskin towels, fresh clothes, strigils, sponges, oil jars, and more. Everyone carried themselves with nonchalant ease; no one seemed bothered by being observed in their natural state.

We strolled through a series of dimly lit corridors, each adorned with frescoes celebrating male beauty: athletes engaged in various competitions, bare-chested peasants toiling in fields and riding horses, fishermen setting their nets. As we traversed a hall with tall windows offering glimpses of the courtyard, I had the impulse to stop and take a closer look; however, Eusebius and Renatus continued onward, so I hastened to catch up with them, not wanting to risk losing my way.

We entered a room suffused with light streaming in through small clerestory windows on all sides. The ceiling had the form of a semicircular barrel vault and was decorated with stucco-painted reliefs with flower and animal motifs. On the walls were a series of niches separated by bearded telamons. Long marble benches surrounded on two sides a central pool filled with water at room temperature. Eusebius ran into acquaintances and sat next to them inside the pool. Renatus and I followed suit. As Eusebius conversed, we sat in an awkward silence, although Renatus's expression showed that he was less uncomfortable than I was. *Calm down, Lucius, and relish in the moment. How many times have you found yourself in the company of so many naked men in such a tranquil setting?* The perfect temperature of the water and the gentle caress of the sun's rays on my skin helped me put my mind at ease.

After some time, Eusebius emerged from the pool and gestured for Renatus and me to follow. We put our sandals and towels back on and headed for the next room, which Renatus told me was the *caldarium*. A cloud of scented steam hit my nose as soon as we stepped in. I couldn't see a thing, so I clung to Renatus's arm for guidance. We eventually reached a broad marble bench and sat down side by side, allowing our eyes to adjust to the dimness. The sole source of light was a brazier with glowing embers. I gradually discerned faint shadows in the darkness.

The room was occupied by about twenty males, yet no conversation was happening. The sound of a small splash of water came from the back. Renatus rose and lightly tapped my arm. I trailed behind him, the ochre and white mosaic floor feeling warm beneath my feet.

"Ouch!" I exclaimed as I dipped my toes into the scalding water.

"Be careful," Renatus whispered.

I dipped my foot in the water once more, this time slowly. I gradually acclimated to the intense heat, and after a few minutes, I could submerge myself fully in the pool, my body discovering a soothing pleasure in the intense heat.

Before long, however, we were back in the *tepidarium*, then outside again. Already frustrated by the constant coming and going, the biting chill that swept over me in the next room was more than I could handle.

"This is ridiculous," I said to Renatus, pointing to the snow inside the pool. "I'm going to freeze to death."

"You're welcome to explore other areas, if you like."

Annoyed, I took him at his word. After procuring a fresh towel, I crossed an arched doorway into the courtyard, where I was momentarily blinded by the harsh rays of the sun.

Before me stretched a dazzling *palaestra*, where athletic men were exercising and playing *follis* in the nude. I sat on one of the wooden benches and leisurely admired their oil-slicked bodies, shimmering with sweat.

There's an allure to the male physique that never fails to captivate me: broad—especially hairy—chests; strong, burly arms; sturdy legs, and well-defined buttocks. Initially, I shamelessly ogled their penises, but as time went on, they ceased to be the primary focus of my attention. A group of young males in playful nudity presents a beauty unmatched in nature. Men are truly the pinnacle of the gods' creation. No wonder we recreate the gods to look like men.

The outdoor pool was also swarming with all kinds of males: young and old, dark- and light-skinned, stocky, and slim, all seemingly enjoying themselves without regard for age, social class, or race distinctions. Some of them invited me to join but I excused myself and retreated indoors.

I moseyed along the corridors until I got lost. I halted to reorient myself, but the convoluted maze of dim, cramped passageways offered no discernible exit path. I eventually came across a door labeled "private." After pushing it open, more of the same dark and narrow corridors followed, but a noticeable difference was the presence of a background sound—an unsettling crescendo of moaning echoing from within the walls.

In an open room, two men lay on padded tables, their naked bodies face down. They were undergoing skilled massages from two adept masseurs, whose rhythmic motions caused the plumpness of the men's buttocks to shake with each deliberate stroke. In an adjoining room, one man was being meticulously scraped with a strigil by a young slave, efficiently removing oil and sweat from his body. Another man was being treated to an aromatic rub-down, with fragrances applied to every inch of his body.

Continuing my exploration, I reached a dry chamber furnished with wooden benches, heated by braziers emanating the fragrant smoke of burning incense sticks. Gentle rays of sunlight filtered through small clerestory windows. The pleasant scent and comfortable temperature beckoned me to linger, so I sat down.

Silhouettes of men—in pairs or in groups of three or four—offered an obscene spectacle as they pleasured each other. An older man was sitting while two young men took turns sucking and licking his cock. Sometimes they would lick it at the same time from both sides, and sometimes one would suck his balls while the other worked on his shaft. The old man leaned his head back in pleasure and pushed the heads of the boys down onto his crotch. Another man standing next to them was jerking off while watching the scene. I untied my towel and started touching myself too.

A man, roughly Eusebius's age, sat beside me. He remained silent for a while and then placed his hand on my left thigh. I was trembling but didn't pull away. He guided my left hand to his cock and wrapped my fingers around it. Instinctively I began to move it up and down, while masturbating my own cock. I slid his foreskin down and touched the head of his dick with the tip of my thumb. I stopped pleasuring myself for a while and massaged his balls with my right hand. His cock became rock hard in an instant. He signaled me to lean over and reach between his thighs with my head. I used on his shaft the skills I had learned with Renatus, with immediate effect. The man let out sighs of pleasure.

After a while, deciding it had been enough, I got up and left the room. I chuckled a little, knowing I had left him on the verge of cumming. I stumbled into another room, full of steam like the *caldarium*, but with a different smell: mint mixed with cum. The action in this room was more intense than in the sauna. One man had bent over, leaning on one of the marble benches and was being penetrated by a man who was slapping his ass as he thrust inside him. The active fucker was also kissing another man.

Then the door opened again. It was the man I had been sucking in the sauna. He positioned himself behind me and started rubbing my butt with his hard cock. At that point I no longer cared, so I leaned forward a bit. He was loosening my towel when the door opened again. Although the steam obscured my vision, I immediately recognized the figure entering: it was Renatus. I hastily straightened up my towel, leaving the man perplexed once more. Renatus turned and left. I exited the room whispering his name, as anything louder than a whisper would have been excessively loud. Holding my towel to keep it in place, I strode the corridors looking for him, but my search was fruitless. I stopped, leaning on a wall. *Why do I feel guilty, when he had made it abundantly clear that "we're just friends"?*

To divert my attention, I followed the moans echoing in the background. Some emanated from a partially open door near me. I cautiously pushed it open a bit further to sneak a peek inside, and to my surprise, there was Eusebius on all fours on a bed, being vigorously penetrated by a white, bald, and strikingly attractive man—likely in his thirties—who sported a stubble and had a strong, smooth, finely sculpted chest. Witnessing Eusebius in this manner, vulnerable, being fucked like a sow, brought me a modicum of pleasure. From his whimpers, I could discern that the cock was too big for his ass, but he was undeniably enjoying the experience.

The man pulled out and jerked off until he released, smearing the fur on Eusebius's lower back. The bald man then glanced in my direction, and startled, I pulled away. I didn't want Eusebius to catch sight of me. Once more, I stopped by the massage room, and this time, the two masseurs were working on their clients' cocks with their hands and mouths. Before long, one of the clients experienced a sudden, explosive release, like a volcanic eruption, his semen cascading on the masseur's hand and all over his stomach. The other client soon followed suit with loud moans. Although the spectacle was entertaining, I resumed walking since I still needed to locate Renatus. I decided to wait for him in the locker room. On my way there, I passed by a grand *triclinium*, where men of high social standing—dressed in fine attire, freshly bathed, anointed, and perfumed—were indulging in a lavish dinner, attended by their servants. It seemed to be a gathering of merchants or politicians; I couldn't really tell.

I reached the *apodyterium* and put on my tunic. Sitting on one of the benches, I waited for Renatus, and my attention was drawn to a particular conversation.

"Is this your first time here in the Stabians?" an attractive middle-aged man asked another, as they disrobed.

"Yes, first time in Pompeii actually, here for business," the other man replied as he wrapped a towel around his waist. He was about the same age and equally handsome, with a robust, very hairy chest. "I'm looking to purchase some imports and have them transported to Capua."

"You're going to love these baths. The facilities are remarkable, among the best in the empire. Plus, there are some additional areas where you can experience true relaxation, if you know what I mean."

"I've heard about that. In fact, that's precisely the reason why I chose these baths. I'm very much in need to relax after such a long journey."

"Are you here by yourself?"

"Just with my servants, but they're waiting outside."

"Excellent. Come with me. You'll be my guest today. I'll show you all there is to see in this place. You won't want to leave."

Huh. So, Pompeii was the place where men from all over the empire came to partake in this kind of "relaxation" experience. I had no idea that there were so many men like me and Renatus, who by the way still hadn't appeared. Had he found someone to mess around with? An uncomfortable sensation stirred in my stomach.

9

I continued visiting the baths. After ignoring me for days, Renatus intercepted me as I was about to leave the house.

"Lucius," he said, gripping my arm. "Can we talk for a moment?"

"About what?" I said, gazing into his eyes.

He led me to the garden, where we sat on a bench.

"Are you going to the baths again?"

"Do you care?"

"I don't—well, yes, I do care." He paused. "What's wrong with you, Lucius?"

"Excuse me?" I said, furrowing my brow. "Hadn't you said I should pursue anything that gives me pleasure? Going to the baths gives me pleasure. A lot," I added with a smirk.

He sighed. "Are you sure you're doing this for pleasure and not out of spite?"

"Do you think I still care about what happened weeks ago? I don't," I lied. "It's in the past, over, and forgotten."

"Then," he said, taking my hand, "why haven't you returned to my bed?"

"Really?" I said, shaking off his grip.

"See? That's proof that you're not alright. You're still holding a grudge against me and my father."

"Your father?"

"Well—Eusebius."

"Is that all you wanted to tell me? Because I'd really like to go now. My friends are waiting for me."

"What friends?"

"Are you my keeper?" I said, rising.

"If you're spending Eusebius's money, you should at least let us know who you're hanging out with."

I shot him an infuriated look and left the house. *Money—of all things, that's what he cares about now?*

I arrived at my destination a few minutes later—not the baths in the city center, but to a *balnea* located on a hill, near the walls, in the southernmost part of Pompeii. A sign at the entrance read "Sarno Baths."

"Hey there, *amice*, you made it," a husky voice greeted me from behind. Hector was a boy my age with whom I had recently made acquaintance. "You're going to enjoy this place. It's got a bit of a kinkier vibe and is way more fun than the Stabians. The people here are cooler and not as uptight."

I hoped he was right. The Stabians were fun, but Hector had a point: the majority of its patrons were older men, and we were both looking forward to exciting times with fellows our own age. Besides, these baths were cheaper. If, as Renatus had remarked, I was spending Eusebius's money, I should at least make sure I got the most out of it.

Obnoxious food vendors, advertising their products each with their characteristic intonation, crammed the sidewalk in front of the entrance. Some patrons were purchasing food to take inside, suggesting that this place didn't have its own dining rooms like the Stabians. Hector and I stood in line among a motley crew of ordinary men, including, of course, some cute boys.

These baths were more modest and not as well maintained. The paint on the walls had faded and, in some places, was completely scuffed. The ceilings were covered in old stucco and with no decorations or statuary. The ambience was gloomy and a bit shabby; it carried a somewhat sketchy vibe. Nevertheless, it meant the beginning of a new, exciting adventure.

The *apodyterium* lacked guards, and instead there was only a bored-looking boy handing locker keys with cords to tie around our arms. We stored our garments and tied towels around our waists.

When I first met Hector at the Stabians, he was working as a servant for a senior man. His role consisted of carrying his belongings and scraping his body with a strigil after bathing. He claimed that the man paid him good money for oral sex, but I didn't personally witness him in action. Hector and I had chatted for a bit while his patron was busy talking to other businessmen in the pool. My new friend was kind of cute: short in height, with tanned skin and short black hair. He didn't hold a candle to Renatus's athletic physique but wasn't bad looking either. More importantly, he was a lot of fun to hang out with; he possessed sharp wit, a clever demeanor, and seemed to have no fear of anything. From the way he spoke, I could tell he belonged to the lower class, but I didn't care.

Our walk took us through the *palaestra*, a space that didn't live up to its name. It was an oddly shaped exercise ground with a small, cramped peristyle tucked away at one end. It had modest decorations, including a wooden colonnade on a stone stylobate. The men exercising there were undeniably hot, though, much more so than those at the Stabians. It was a pleasure to see their well-endowed cocks swaying and jiggling as they played ball.

We eventually arrived at the swimming pool, which left much to be desired; the water needed to be changed more frequently.

Some of the men playing ball in the pool invited us to join. It was a scorching day, so the refreshing plunge was absolutely fantastic. I felt more invigorated than I had in months. *What an amazing experience to be surrounded by so many hunks who just want to have fun, and treat you like a friend.*

After some time in the pool, we headed indoors, navigating through dim and rundown corridors. Some damage from the earthquake years before had yet to be repaired. Certain passageways had deteriorated to a perilous state, displaying significant transversal cracks. The ceiling looked like it was going to collapse. Still, nobody seemed concerned about its dilapidated condition.

We entered the small and cramped *caldarium*—nowhere near as hot as the one in the Stabians. It lacked a *hypocaustum*, so the mosaic floors felt cold underfoot. We stayed there just long enough to raise our body temperature before continuing down the corridors until we reached a sauna, where a peculiar smell, sweet and pungent at the same time, filled the air. Hector sat on one of the wooden benches, legs brushing with a middle-aged man, and I sat next to Hector. The man offered my friend a wooden plate covered by a felt tent, with a hole on top from which smoke emanated.

Hector took a puff. "Try this," he said to me, "you're going to love it."

My puff was followed by a cough.

"Easy, boy." The man chuckled. "Do it slowly."

I gave it a second try, letting the scented smoke warm me up inside.

"Do you like it?" Hector asked.

"Yeah, what is it?"

"It's called cannabis. It's pretty expensive stuff." He leaned in closer and whispered in my ear, "This is not the best quality, but it will do to get you high." We chuckled.

"Cannabis. Never heard of it," I said. "But it sure feels great."

I leaned my back and head against the wooden wall. Everything around seemed so beautiful, and a deep sense of joy swathed me. I found myself wishing Renatus could experience this with me. I even wished Eusebius was present too.

I felt a tickle in my inner thighs. I glanced down, and found the man down on his knees, sucking my dick. It was an amazing sensation I hadn't experienced before. Even Renatus had never done this to me, but now I understood why he liked having his dick sucked so much. The man's tongue glided effortlessly up and down my shaft, and its tip lick the watery hole of my cock head, sending shivers of pleasure through me.

Hector put his arm around me and kissed me. Without comparing him to Renatus, he was a great kisser, and I delighted in the expert sliding of his tongue inside my mouth.

The man moved on to Hector's cock. My friend leaned back and closed his eyes, enjoying the mastery of the work being performed on him. After a while, the stranger returned to my cock. He sucked me while he jerked Hector off, and then the other way around. I had to lightly pat him on the head to get him to stop; I wasn't ready to cum yet.

Hector and I ventured further into the building, navigating the dimly lit corridors lined with *cubicula*. Some of these rooms had no doors, not even beaded curtains, allowing one to witness the activities transpiring inside. We reached a smaller section that resembled a maze. In one of the subdivisions, there was a hammock-looking contraption, crafted from leather and suspended from a wooden frame by sturdy ropes and metal rings.

"What's this for?" I asked.

Hector lay on it and spread his legs over the ropes. "This is how you lie down here."

"Can I try?"

"Sure," he said, standing up.

I lay down like him, resting my legs on the ropes, scratching me a little. My hole got wide open, right in front of my partner. *An invitation, I guess.*

"Do you want me to… fuck you?"

"Yeah." I hadn't had cock since that last time with Eusebius, and I wanted to get that impression out of my head. This felt like a good opportunity to start over.

He leaned in front of me and spat on his growing cock. I felt the pressure of his head stretching my hole. A crowd of onlookers quickly gathered around us. He kept pushing gently, until his whole manhood was inside me. My hole throbbed as it got used to the foreign presence. He moved slowly, without pulling his cock all the way out, and after a few minutes he had picked up a good pace and was slamming my buttocks with his thighs. *What an incredible sensation.* Some of the men around us inhaled cannabis while stroking their cocks. Some kissed each other.

"Do you want to do something fun?" Hector asked.

"Yeah."

"Get up."

I did it, a little confused. Did he want me to fuck him? *I'm not really into that.*

"Get on top of me," he said as he lay down on the sling. "We're going to do something that's going to boggle your mind."

I placed my back against his chest, still not quite understanding what he wanted to do. He asked me to get comfortable so he could fuck me in that position. I moved up a little, as he directed his hard cock to my asshole with his hand, and soon his shaft was entering me, a little easier this time.

"Do you want to feel two cocks inside?" he whispered.

That sounded like a pretty wild idea, and perhaps under other conditions I wouldn't have done it, but I was feeling adventurous, so I nodded.

"Any of you want to join us?" he asked the group around us.

"Hell, yeah!" one of them replied.

Hector pulled me back, still propping my ass open with his cock. Soon after, I felt the slippery thrust of another member inside.

"By Hercules!" I exclaimed, the enormous pressure tearing up my hole. "Please, don't move. Stay inside me for a while."

"Are you alright?" Hector asked.

"Yes, I just need to get used to it."

A little later, the man asked, "Ready now?"

"Yeah," I said with a sigh.

Both resumed pounding me, stretching my hole like never before. The slick motion of the two cocks was fantastic, like two snakes making out inside me.

Soon the man's gush warmed my guts. He pulled out as Hector continued to slide in, taking advantage of the extra lubrication.

"Who wants to be next?" Hector asked.

Another man joined in. I had grown even hungrier for two cocks inside my hole. I moaned loudly when I felt the incoming pressure, exciting the banter of the men around us.

One of them gave me his cock to suck. A third man entered me after the second one cummed. And then a fourth, and a fifth. I lost track of how many men enjoyed my hole and how many dicks I tasted.

"Fuck, man, I'm going to cum!" Hector exclaimed. "I can't hold it any longer." Moaning loudly, he ejaculated, his seed mixing with the milk that all the other men had left inside me. "Now, I'll make you release your load," he said, grabbing my cock and frantically jerking it off.

Like a fountain, I splashed my seed all over my abdomen and legs. Two men leaned down and licked me all over. Hector turned my head and kissed me.

Panting, we stayed in the sling for a few more moments, while a strong rush of heat ran through my head, giving me the magical sensation of traveling to another world.

10

Hector and I continued visiting the Stabian Baths. Sometimes he would ask me to watch him perform *fellatio* on his clients, but for me it was hottest when he groomed them—strigiling them after a hot bath, trimming their body hair, or anointing them with oil or perfume.

This time, he was busy with a customer who had solicited him for sex in private, and I found myself alone, just wandering about. A little hungry, I headed to the *apodyterium* to dry off and change into my clothes before going out to grab a snack. As I stepped onto the street, I ran into a familiar-looking man waiting in line. He fixed his gaze on me, arching his eyebrows. I turned around, hugging myself pretending to be cold. Retracing my steps, I concealed myself behind a corner, waiting for him to enter the *apodyterium*. Once he was out of sight, I hurried out of the premises. All the way home, I had the strange feeling of being watched, as if now everyone in Pompeii knew who I was.

In the two weeks that followed, Hector and I had sex at the Sarnos a few times—in public because we couldn't afford a private room—but without other men joining in. I never went back to the Stabians, making excuses every time Hector invited me.

This afternoon I was at the Sarnos on my own, as Hector had to work at the Stabians. I couldn't find peace in Eusebius's *domus*, so I avoided being there as much as possible. I increasingly felt like an imposition on him and his family, especially due to my own escalating absurd behavior. I would have been willing to change if they had requested, but their detachment, verging on indifference, deeply irritated me.

Craving for a bit of excitement, I walked in rounds down the aisles along the *cubicula*, not-so-subtly seeking a partner. A man, likely in his fifties, gestured for me to come with him. I'm not that much into older men, but I was feeling bored, and he was an attractive fellow for his age. He took me by the hand and led me down the halls to an area I hadn't explored before.

We entered a door I thought to be permanently closed, and suddenly found ourselves out in the street, in a desolate alley. Frightened, I told him that I would prefer to stay inside, but then he clamped his hand over my mouth and pinned my arm behind my back. Before long, he forcefully led me into a *carpentum* where two other men bound my hands, blindfolded me, and silenced me with a gag. They seated themselves on either side of me, and the coach moved away. *This is the end of me.*

After a while, the vehicle stopped amid an eerie silence. The men carried me up multiple flights of stairs. A key unlocked a door. They took me inside a cold, musty-smelling room and threw me on the floor. They removed the blindfold, but the room was dark. With that, they departed, locking the door behind them. I wept, realizing I had lost my freedom, the only thing I had left, since my dignity was long gone.

Hunger and thirst plagued me, and I didn't know whether it was day or night. A key turned in the lock. A man carrying a candle entered the room—the same man who had seduced me in the baths. He squatted down in front of me and loosened my gag.

"How are you feeling?" he asked with a smirk.

"Why did you bring me here? I was going to lie with you willingly."

"I know you were, you little slut. But that wasn't what I wanted."

"Then what is it?"

"Shhh! If you scream, I'll put the gag back on. Not that anyone can hear you here anyway. As you may have noticed, we're in a pretty secluded part of town."

"Please, have mercy!"

"Don't worry, boy. You won't be doing anything you don't like."

I frowned.

"I was one of the men who bred you at the Sarnos," he said with a sarcastic smile. "You're such a hungry pig. You liked having all those men inside you, didn't you? That's why I thought you'd enjoy being here."

"I… don't understand."

"You like to fuck, don't you? Here you will be fucking a lot but making me money as you do it. I'll hook you up with clients who will visit you in this room; I'll get the silver and you'll get the cock you crave so much, and maybe some food every once in a while."

My body shuddered in terror. Everything became a blur.

"If you behave yourself, I'll treat you well. You enjoyed my cock, right?" he said with a chuckle. "I hope you did, because I will also use you for my private amusement when your visitors are done with you."

He lifted his tunic, grabbed his cock, and showed me his balls.

"Come on, take a lick."

I turned my head away in disgust.

He laughed. "I see you're not in the mood. Just to show you how good I am, I'll allow you some rest for now. But tomorrow, you'd better be ready to cater to my clients."

"May I please have something to eat?"

"Tomorrow. This will give you ample time to contemplate the advantages of compliance."

He placed the gag again while I shook and screamed.

Sleep eluded me all night. My mind searched fruitlessly for a way out. Exhaustion only took hold of me first thing in the morning.

A nightmare startled me awake soon after. Standing on top of Mount Vesuvius, a powerful earthquake sent me tumbling down the slope, causing me to crash and break my bones. The pain felt real, but it was simply the result of my uncomfortable sleeping position.

A few slivers of sunlight slipped through the cracks in the wooden window shutters, as noises at the door signaled someone coming in. A man approached me without a word, removed my gag, and untied my hands. He put a plate and a goblet of water in front of me and left. It was *puls* on the brink of spoiling, but I devoured it like food of gods. Some time later, my captor entered the room.

"I see that you've eaten all your meal. Very good. You'll need energy to meet your first customer today."

"But *domine*, I feel disgusting. Could you provide me with a basin so I wash myself?"

"What do you take this place for, a *caupona*? Don't be ridiculous, boy. You were in the baths just yesterday. Besides, my client likes the smell of fresh sweat." He approached me and sniffed me like a dog. "In fact, I'm starting to feel rather turned on myself," he said, grabbing his crotch.

I shuddered at the prospect of seeing his hairy balls again.

"Take a nap if you want. You'll have company tonight."

I lay on the floor, awaiting my fate, every part of my body aching. After endless hours, the door creaked open and my captor ushered an old man into the room.

"There he is. He's submissive and compliant. Use him in whatever manner you please," he said to him before leaving.

The old man, fat and clumsy, his head covered only by a half-circle of disheveled white hair, squatted down in front of me.

"You really are a nice boy," he said, touching my chin. "Albus wasn't lying." He ran his fingers through my hair, causing me to recoil. "I can't let people know of my preferences, so I must resort to captives to satisfy my needs. I hope you don't mind." He stood up and loosened his belt. "Why don't you... get down on your knees and start attending to me."

I must think quickly. Albus—now I knew his name—hadn't locked the door. I didn't think he would be waiting outside. He was counting on me being too feeble or too frightened to try anything.

"Could you please... sit down and lean against the wall, *domine*? It would make it easier for me to service you and you'll be more comfortable."

"You've got manners as well," he said, patting my head. "Maybe we can have a pleasant conversation once we're done."

He sat up with a groan. *Great. He'll have a hard time getting up.*

"Close your eyes, *domine*. I'm about to do something you'll never forget."

He closed his eyes and lifted up his robe, unveiling his flaccid penis. I didn't even get a good look at it because I was getting ready to give him the surprise of his life.

Summoning all my strength, I delivered a powerful punch to his balls. The poor bastard groaned in agony and collapsed to the side, unconscious.

I hurriedly got to my feet and dashed to the door. After a brief check in both directions down the dimly lit hallway, I discerned no one in sight. I moved stealthily in the dark, searching for the stairs leading to the first floor. The front door was locked from the outside. I let out a whispered curse and paced back and forth. A potted plant was near the door.

Later, a key turned in the lock. In a hasty move, I slipped behind the door, lifting the heavy pot. I struck the man over the head and delivered a kick to his groin. He went down—I didn't wait to confirm if it was Albus or not—and I fled the building. Well aware of the perils of the night streets in any Roman city, I moved without a specific direction, though no place could be more dangerous than where I was.

I ran until I found a straw cart in an alley. I curled up inside, hoping to regain my strength, but sleep remained elusive. My heart was still racing, and my mind refused to stop thinking.

After the first birdsong at dawn, people started passing by, so I came out of my hiding and asked them where I was and how to get to the center.

A few hours later, I stood at the doorstep of Eusebius's *domus* and knocked on the door.

"Good heavens, Lucius!" Renatus exclaimed as he opened the door. "Where have you been? We've been looking all over for you."

I crumbled into his arms, tears streaming down my face.

"Mom, he's back!" he shouted as he carried me to my room.

"Oh dear, I'm so glad." Gaia rushed toward me and planted a kiss on my cheek. "Have some rest, honey. I'll cook a hearty soup for you."

In my room, between sobs I tried to explain to Renatus everything that had happened, but he stopped me.

"Don't stress, precious. We'll have time to talk later. You're safe now. Please sleep a little. The smell of my mom's soup is sure to wake you up."

11

For several days, I was too scared to leave the house. Renatus was now insisting that I tell him what had happened, but I couldn't bring myself to. After it had been echoing in my mind for so long, it all felt too embarrassing, too humiliating to recount. I was certain he knew it was connected to my ventures in the shady Sarno baths, but he never uttered an "I told you," even though he had the right to do so.

Gaia came to my room while Eusebius and Renatus were not home.

"Darling, I'm heading to the market for groceries. Will you come with me?"

Sweet Gaia, always trying to cheer me up. This was the first time she had invited me to accompany her since my return. Perhaps she sensed that the time was right.

"Sure. Can you give me a minute to change my clothes?"

"I'll be in the garden. Take your time, honey."

I wished she were my mother. I never received that kind of treatment from her.

"See?" she said when I joined her in the garden, where she was watering her petunias. "All they need is a little water and lots of sunshine, and they're sure to bloom and grace us with their beauty."

I smiled. She took two cloth grocery bags and handed one to me, attaching a money pouch to her belt.

The beautiful sunny morning, refreshed by an invigorating see breeze, made me feel so good to be outdoors again, to slowly leave fear behind. Everything that had occurred began to fade away like a bad dream. I was back with my adoptive family, I had a roof over my head and enough to eat, I was free… What more could I wish for? Even the night with Renatus and Eusebius had started to transform into a distant memory. Renatus and I were talking again, and things were almost like the old days, although we had not yet resumed our physical intimacy. This time it had nothing to do with him or Eusebius, but everything to do with the traumatic experience of my abduction.

Shoppers endeavored to choose the best quality produce, and vendors grumbled, urging them not to handle items too much if they weren't going to purchase them. The sound of coins exchanged for goods echoed through the surroundings.

"Look at this spelt, dear. Doesn't it look wonderful? I'm going to get some of it. I'm certain it will make scrumptious bread."

Gaia seemed delighted in shopping. She could have easily delegated the task to one of her slaves, but it was evident that it was also a form of amusement for her—perhaps one of those "simple pleasures" they talked so much about.

"Will you help me pick out a few apples and pears?" she said, passing me a basket. "I'm going to check the cucumbers."

My attention was captured by a stout man who scanned the market with a menacing bearing. Panic gripped my heart, fearing that he might be searching for me. Discreetly, I placed the apples back in their place and backtracked stealthily, attempting to creep out of the market unnoticed.

After I had gone a few steps, I turned my back on him and quickened my pace, weaving through barrels of olives, crates of figs, and stalls of hot spices.

As I neared an exit, I turned and found his gaze locking onto mine. My heart thudded in terror. Without a second thought, I dropped the basket onto the cobblestone ground and sprinted away, gasping for breath. In my frantic haste, I stumbled over a couple of stalls. Apples collided with melons and plums scattered like marbles in a colorful chaos. One old seller, his face flushed and his hands trembling with rage, looked helplessly to the disheartening scene.

"Watch where you're going, you imbecile!" he shouted at me.

Others joined him, cursing me for my clumsiness in Latin and several dialects. I stammered out apologies as I cast a quick glance back, anxious to see if my pursuer was closing in. My heart leaped when I spotted him moving through the chaos in my direction. There was no time to lose.

When I reached the street, I sprinted into a throng of people, trying to fool my chaser. Running block after block, veering left and right, I arrived at the open space of the forum. The *macellum* in front of it offered the perfect sanctuary to shake off my relentless chaser.

The vendors' shouting, proclaiming their wares to anyone within earshot, echoed long before I reached the entrance. A briny mix of raw meat and fish odors hit my nostrils intensely as soon as I entered. I pushed my way through the crowd, seeking shelter amid the varied assortment of meats, which ranged from boar and venison to duck and geese.

In a second episode of clumsiness, I accidentally knocked over a display of glistening silver fish, causing them to flop and slide across the ground, and later another stall, this time laden with cured meats and sausages. With no time to apologize, I hurriedly continued my escape amid the exasperated insults of the vendors. The man was still after me.

I dashed out of the *macellum* through the opposite side, and I kept running as fast as my legs could carry me, altering my direction at every intersection until I finally reached Eusebius's *domus*. I knocked frantically on the door, and as soon as one of the slaves opened, I dashed inside and sought refuge in my room, where I curled up in bed and remained there for hours.

Gaia came to see me as soon as she returned home.

"My dear, what happened? What did you see that frightened you so much?"

"It was a man... a man, Gaia. He wanted to take me away."

"Did you know him at all?"

I had no alternative but to tell her what had happened to me during the days I had been missing. She listened with empathy and genuine concern.

"Then... do you think that this man is connected to the gang that abducted you?"

"I don't know. He might..."

"You mentioned that you found out the name of their leader, correct? What was it?"

"Albus... yes, Albus, I believe."

"I'm going to speak with Eusebius about arranging an investigation. We need to find out who these people are and get help in dismantling their operations."

"But that must be hard, Gaia. I'm certain many of their clients must be affluent men in high positions. I don't think there's much we can do about it."

"Then you should start carrying a dagger with you."

"A dagger?"

"You're being targeted!"

"I'll consider it. But for now, I think it's best for me to stay home. Maybe after a few weeks they'll forget about me."

"Weeks? You can't live in fear, darling." She paused for a moment. "If you're afraid to go out by yourself, have Renatus or Eusebius accompany you. They won't dare attack you if you're with them."

In the days that followed, that's exactly what I did. But I still couldn't shake the unsettling feeling that we were being watched every time we left the house.

"I believe someone followed us," I confided in Renatus after we returned from a tavern.

"How do you know that? Did you see anyone?"

"No. But, I can feel it."

"Lucius, please. You're still shaken by the whole ordeal. Besides, no one would dare to harm you I'm with you; I'd beat the shit out of that sucker."

I smiled, clinging to his arm. It was reassuring to hear his words, and I felt safe with him. But I also feared for the family. I didn't want them to get in trouble with criminals on my account. We didn't know how far these people would go to get me back, or to silence me.

Sometimes they left home alone when they went out for business. This morning, I was trying to combat boredom by perusing one of the numerous scrolls in the library, although I couldn't really comprehend much of what I was reading. The text I selected had to do with the minuscule particles called "atoms," which Renatus had mentioned during our studies. Pretty heavy stuff, filled with lots of unintelligible Greek terms. But I went ahead and kept reading.

'If there is motion, there is void. There is motion. Therefore, there is void,' one of the paragraphs read. *Alright, I get that.* Those are the only two things that exist, according to this book: atoms and voids. I kept reading. *'All the things we experience with the senses are nothing but different arrangements of atoms and voids, which as such, exist only for a limited time, until random movements arrange them in other forms. But atoms themselves are eternal and indivisible.'* The scroll went on to explain that *'when a cow defecates, atoms of*

the food it ate are deposited in the soil, which is then used by plants to grow, and which in turn are eaten by other beings and becomes a part of them. Atoms are also moved by forces of nature; mountains are eroded by the wind, rivers change their course over the years, fire destroys forests, but in the end, all the basic components of nature remain somewhere in the world and end up becoming part of something else.'

I put the scroll down to meditate. So, has the world always existed? The papyrus provided a definitive answer. Yes. I went on to read how the properties of things such as their smell, taste, and shape, were the properties of the aggregates themselves and not of the atoms, which in essence are all the same. It also explained how in this eternal motion of atoms there were collisions that gave rise to the existence of these aggregates. It introduced the concept of "swerve" in which atoms occasionally stray from their natural path, and— the manuscript promised—*'it will be explained later how this leads to the concept of free will, and why we, as humans, have a say in our destiny, which is neither the product of the will of the gods nor the result entirely of chance.'*

We have a say in our destiny. I stared at a blank space. *I want to have a say. I want to decide my own future.*

Engrossed in these thoughts, a knock from the street-facing door startled me. Normally, I would have let a slave open it, but I felt brave enough to do it myself.

The sight that greeted me turned me to stone.

"*Salve*, Lucius," the man before me said. Dressed in a pristine toga and an opulent white linen tunic, he stood still for a few moments, gazing at me with an impassive face. "Can we talk?"

12

I gestured for him to come inside, trying to conceal the trembling of my hands.

The man walked slowly, taking his time inspecting the house. "Nice home. I'd imagined you'd be somewhere much rougher."

"Or dead?"

"Or dead," he confirmed, fixing the gaze of his deep green eyes on me.

I ushered him into the library.

"What's this?" he said, picking up one of the scrolls. "Have you been studying? These had better be law books."

"They're philosophy books," I said, taking it from his grasp. "Why are you here, Father?"

"Aren't you happy to see me?"

"After I ran away from home?"

"Your mother has been deadly worried," he said, as I motioned for us to take a seat. "We've been looking for you everywhere. All your friends said they knew nothing of your whereabouts."

"I didn't tell anyone. I don't intend this to be temporary."

"Who are these people you're staying with?"

"They're good people."

"Do I know them?"

"I doubt it. They're not in your... circle."

"I still can't believe you made it all the way to Pompeii. The pomegranate picker informed us of your actions. We organized a search squad around Mount Vesuvius and the neighboring farms and villas. No one reported having sighted you, which seemed very strange to me. A stripling like you wouldn't know how to fend for himself in the woods."

"I'm not a stripling anymore. I'm eighteen."

"Then start behaving like a man and don't run away from your responsibilities."

"But I don't want responsibilities. I want to be free to live the life I choose."

"That, my Son," he said, standing up, "is a privilege that not even the Caesars have."

I stood up too. "How did you find me?"

"One of my colleagues saw you here in Pompeii. Afterward, I paid men to search the city and discover your hideout."

The man in the baths—I should have anticipated he'd be a talker. Would he also have told my father where he saw me?

"You're coming back with me right now."

"I'm staying here."

He sighed with impatience.

"Accept it, Father. I don't live in your house anymore."

"As you wish," he said before exiting the library. "But there will be consequences."

I trailed behind him. "Now you know where I am. Go away and tell my mother that I'm fine and that I love her, but I'm not coming back home."

He was making his way toward the front door when Eusebius and Renatus arrived. Spotting him, they both gazed at me in bewilderment. Eusebius extended his hand, but my father responded with a disdainful expression on his face.

"You'll be hearing from me."

"Who was that?" Eusebius asked. I remained silent. "We have much to discuss, young man."

"Isn't it obvious? That's his father." Renatus turned to me. "Let me guess, he wants you to go back home?"

"Yes, but I'm not going to."

"Perhaps it's time for you to share the whole story with us," Eusebius said.

In the library, I began by revealing the name of my father, Lucius Cornelius Successianus, a prominent Neapolitan lawyer with a reputation in legal circles, especially for the ruthless manner in which he handled his cases, which earned him numerous resounding victories. I described my upbringing in the bosom of a well-to-do family, residing in a grand *domus* nestled in the heart of Neapolis. My mother, of old Patrician heritage, held a central role in our exclusive social circle. In contrast, my father, an *homo novus*, had gained much from his marriage to her. He was embittered by the fact that many within my mother's class viewed him as an upstart, despite his legal prowess. Regrettably, I had no siblings, which left me as the sole focus of my family's attention.

"Your father's name certainly sounds familiar," Eusebius said. "Then Cornelius is your real family name, right?"

"Yes. My full name is Lucius Cornelius Abercius."

"I still don't understand," Renatus said. "From what you've told us, it doesn't sound like there was a reason for you to run away. I mean, it's not like you already knew the philosophy. What Roman would flee from a life of wealth and prestige?"

"There's a reason when all that wealth and prestige come at a price."

"What price?"

Gaia entered the library. "Why are you gathered here? You look as though you've just seen a ghost."

"In a way we have," I said. "A ghost from the past."

"His father was here," Eusebius said, "and Lucius is finally telling us his life story."

"I'll sit for that," Gaia said. "But before, I'll ask a slave to bring us refreshments."

We brought her up to date while the slave brought goblets of warm honeyed milk.

"So, what's the issue?" she asked, taking a sip.

"He wants me to become a lawyer. And I hate it. I lack the aptitude for words."

"I'm well aware of that." Renatus chuckled. "Though I give you credit for trying to absorb the philosophy into your head," he said, pointing at the papyruses on the table.

"Philosophy is far more appealing than all that legal jargon. Terms, clauses, jurisprudence; I can't stand any of it.

I'd rather face death than immerse myself in it. I want to be an artist!"

"An artist?" Renatus questioned, scratching his head. "But you don't have any talent in that realm, at least, none that I've noticed."

"Don't be hard on Lucius," Gaia said. "We'll allow him the time to discover his true passion." She approached me, taking my hand. "But there's more to this, am I right, sweetheart?"

I nodded.

"What is it then?"

"My father wants me to marry." A brief silence hung in the air. "He expects me to wed a woman I've never even met."

"Come on, Lucius," Gaia said with a chuckle. "We women aren't that dreadful." Her laughter changed to a smile when she noticed my troubled countenance. "I'm just joking, honey. I completely understand," she said, casting a meaningful glance at Renatus. "Don't worry, Lucius, we'll support you. As long as you remain under our roof, he won't be able to force you into anything."

"You don't know my father; he's a very dangerous man. He has connections everywhere, in Neapolis and Rome, and he surely knows magistrates and politicians here too."

"Don't worry about us," Eusebius said. "We know how to protect ourselves."

"You really don't understand... we're all in serious trouble. I... I'd better leave, find somewhere else to stay and keep you all out of this."

"You won't do such a thing," Renatus said, drawing near me and placing his arm around my shoulder.

"I have a suggestion," Gaia said. "How about sending him to Herculaneum for a while? He can find solace in a rural getaway with our acquaintances there."

"And he can delve deeper into the philosophy, not just from a theoretical standpoint, but through practical communal experiences," Renatus said.

"That's a great idea," Eusebius said. "I'll make arrangements."

Book Three

13

In less than a week, I joined a group of Eusebius's acquaintances traveling to Herculaneum. After a few hours on the road, during which we engaged in amicable conversation and enjoyed some provisions, we arrived in the town. Many opulent villas graced its hills, offering splendid vistas of the sea around the shore, with Mount Vesuvius in the background. The specific destination where they would drop me off for the week was a quaint countryside retreat located outside the walls, surrounded by many acres of lush, hilly terrain.

After a friendly welcome, I was led to an outdoor area adjacent to the villa where the initial sessions would be held. There I was introduced to the other participants, a total of around thirty individuals of diverse ages, all over eighteen and of both sexes. The weather was cool and cloudy, which created a comfortable environment for sitting on the large rocks arranged in concentric semicircles on the grass that served as benches.

A lady in her thirties, dressed comfortably in a white robe overlaid with a plain rose-colored stola, addressed the audience.

"Dear guests," she announced loud and clear, "my name is Diana and I welcome you to the Garden of Wisdom and Happiness."

An old woman seated beside me explained to me that all the establishments dedicated to the study of Epicurean Philosophy were called "gardens."

"I'm aware that some of you have just arrived from Pompeii," she said, looking in my direction, "and others came last night from various cities and provinces. Could each of you please introduce yourselves and mention your place of origin?"

When it was my turn, I simply said, "Lucius, from Pompeii."

"Very good," she said. "Now I'd like to ask you a question. How many of you have already familiarized yourselves with the basics of the philosophy? Show of hands, please."

I hesitated for a moment and chose not to raise my hand. I didn't feel like I knew enough.

"Alright," she said, after only a few hands went up. "In that case, I assume everyone would be comfortable if we start with the fundamental principles, for the benefit of the novices?"

Several yeses came from the audience.

"Let me start by explaining what the world is made of. The world, as we know it, is made of tiny, indivisible particles called 'atoms.'"

Oh no, not those damn atoms.

"Don't worry," she said, noting our anxious expressions. "I won't bore you with the intricacies of the physics. That belongs in a more advanced lesson. For now, I'll provide only a few clarifications."

Some of the ideas she introduced sounded familiar from my self-guided studies.

"It may take minutes, days, weeks, years, or centuries, but in the end, everything that exists in a particular form eventually ceases to be, and only its fundamental constituents continue to transform into other things, in an unending cycle, as it has always been."

She delved into the concept of "swerve," which I had been studying at home before my father's interruption. Intriguing, but still went over my head.

"Therefore, if all that exists is matter and void, we can reach our first important conclusion. Does anyone know what it is?"

"That death is nothing to us," one man responded.

Those words resonated in my head as the first time Renatus had pronounced them.

"That is true; that's the first and one of the most important teachings of the master. When we are here, death is not; and when death is here, we are not."

"But what about the spirit," another man inquired. "Where does it go when we die?"

"Nowhere. The spirit doesn't exist. All that exists is what we perceive through our senses. The rest is just an illusion. An illusion that wicked men take advantage of to frighten the ignorant."

The attendees commented among themselves.

"Can anyone tell me the second conclusion?"

"That we should not fear the gods."

"Wonderful! This group is more advanced than I anticipated. I might have to promote you all to the next class."

The attendees laughed.

"We need not fear the gods, dear friends, for our lives and destinies are not subject to their caprices. If they exist, they do not care about us, poor mortals, but do you know what's more likely?" she said in a mocking, whispered tone. "That they do not exist at all."

I heard Gaia's voice in my head saying those words.

"That affirmation troubles me," an elderly man remarked. "Do you really not fear the gods, and that they can punish us at their whim?"

"Not at all," Diana said. "And to prove it, I'll give you a demonstration."

She gestured to two boys, who seemed accustomed to her upcoming actions. They brought a clay bust with the effigy of a bearded old man.

"Do you recognize this?" she inquired, holding it up for all to see.

"That's a bust of Jupiter."

"Exactly, and do you know what I'm going to do with it?"

Before the audience could respond, she raised the statue high into the air and forcefully smashed it against one of the rocks, causing it to shatter into pieces. Gasps of astonishment followed.

"Come on, mighty Jupiter!" she cried out to the sky. "Send lightning to obliterate me. I curse you, and I spit in your face," she declared, acting on her words.

She stood there for a moment, hands on her hips, gazing up at the sky.

"I'm waiting," she said in a whimsical tone, eliciting nervous laughter from some of the attendees.

I shivered. I had never witnessed such a brazen act of desecration. In Neapolis, she would have faced exile. I was in disbelief that this behavior was tolerated in Herculaneum.

"Come on, bring more," she beckoned to the boys.

The youths brought images of Venus, Minerva, Mars, Apollo, and various *lares* and nymphs, which she distributed among the learners to destroy. Some hesitated, but eventually, all of us got hold of at least one image; mine was of Apollo. It saddened me because I had always cherished the god. When I smashed it against the rock that had been serving as my seat, I felt as if I had truly lost my innocence, even more than after that first sexual act with Renatus.

"Look at this," one man said, as he pulled out his cock and pissed on the remnants of the statue he had shattered.

"I can do better," another said, also exposing his cock and stroking it rapidly in front of everyone.

"Let's leave that for another time," Diana said with a chuckle. "You can do whatever you want later, but right now we must move on to the next topic."

I was in a state of utter shock; I had not anticipated anything remotely like this. What I thought would be a tranquil and somewhat boring retreat, had turned out to be quite exciting, if perhaps a little unsettling.

Following a simple lunch of bread with olive oil and dried fruits, Diana announced that the upcoming sessions would be divided into three groups, and new participants would join. There would be a session exclusively for men, one for women, and one mixed-sex assembly, allowing us to choose the one that suited us best. I naturally opted for the men-only meeting.

A man around forty years old, with some remaining curly light brown locks, dressed in a white tunic with a brown drape, welcomed us beneath the shade of a generous umbrella pine tree, as the clouds dissipated, and the sun now beamed brightly in the middle of the sky.

"Welcome, dear men," he began in a calm and pleasant tone, "my name is Artemius. For the sake of the new acquaintances, I would like to kindly request that each of you reintroduce yourselves." We obliged. "In this session," he went on, "you will learn the sole purpose of a man's life."

Now, that piqued my interest. Not even my most insightful childhood tutors had ventured to claim knowledge of what that purpose might be.

"Does anyone here already know the answer?" he asked to no response. "Come on, don't let me down," he said with a grin. "Diana told me that you were an enlightened lot."

It's ironic for her name to be Diana, given the disdain she feels for the goddess.

"The pursuit of happiness."

"So, she didn't deceive me," Artemius said. "I will just add one detail to that proposition: The pursuit of happiness *by means of pleasure* is indeed the sole purpose of life on Earth." He looked at the attendees and stretched out his hands. "I can see from your expressions that some of you are unconvinced, but by the end of this session, I will ensure that not only are you all convinced, but you will also be well-versed in this matter." He paused and paced a little before us. "Everyone knows what pleasure is; I don't need to explain it. However, one thing you might not be aware of, or at least not entirely, is that pleasure follows desire, and desire comes in three different types."

Oh no, definitions again.

"Those three types are: first, natural and necessary; second, natural but unnecessary; and third, unnatural and unnecessary."

My head is spinning.

"Please provide examples of the three," one said.

Artemius adopted a resonant, teacher-like voice. "The first type, that is, natural and necessary, is quite easy to define," he began. "It encompasses of what the body requires to function, such as eating, sleeping, or defecating." He paused. "Men cannot live without these desires, but there are

111

natural limits to them; the stomach gets full, the body awakens after a good night's rest, and there's only so much shit that can come out of one's anus."

The entire gathering burst into laughter.

"We can elaborate more on this later, but for now, I'd like to move on to the third category, that of unnatural and unnecessary desires. These can take three forms: fame, money, and power."

Lightning struck me. Was this man suggesting that everything my family cherished was vain and empty?

"Yes, my dear friends, I understand that it may be difficult for some to accept, but if you are genuinely seeking happiness, you must renounce the pursuit of these three desires, for they are not necessary and have no satiety; there is never enough of any of them, and one remains perpetually consumed by the desire for more, leading to an unhappy life."

Hearing those words had already awakened a certain happiness in my heart—a confirmation of something I had always sensed within.

"The second type of desire is a bit more complex to define," Artemius continued. "It has to do with the first category but in a distorted manner. Let me put it this way— which of these meals do you find more appetizing: a plate of lentils or a turbot seasoned with spices and garum?"

"The turbot," the men said unanimously.

"This is where you're wrong. It will take time, but as you progress further in the philosophy, you'll come to enjoy lentil soup just as much, if not more, than the fanciest of dishes."

"Why is this important?" someone inquired.

"Because, while there is a limit to the capacity of your stomach, there is no limit to the extravagance of your meals. In the same way as desires from the third category, there will always be a more delectable dish, and this, your craving for exquisite foods is insatiable and will evolve into an unending pursuit that will lead to unhappiness."

The men nodded in agreement.

"Where does sex fit into these categories?" one man asked.

"I was expecting that question," Artemius said with a chuckle. "Sex, my dear friend, falls into the second category, for while it is necessary if you want to have offspring, it can also become an obsession, for it has no limits in its forms and varieties."

Exclamations of disappointment followed.

"So sex is only necessary for procreation?" the man inquired.

"That's right. It's not like you're going to die if you don't have sex."

"I'm not so sure about that," a voice in the background chimed in, prompting laughter.

"But don't be disheartened, my fellow men. It is not my duty to deprive you of these pleasures. It is solely your choice to decide if and when you wish to embrace chastity. Only a few of the most advanced and dedicated learners opt for this path. But they don't reprimand themselves if they occasionally partake in those pleasures along the way because—contrary to what some are preaching out there—no one is obligated to attain ideals of perfection."

"In fact," he added with a smile, "I encourage you to explore your sexual curiosities if they are burning within you. There are techniques that can teach you how to experience far greater pleasure than just engaging in sexual relations with another person. In fact, solitary sex can lead to the most profound satisfaction, as you are always in control and can closely heed your body's signals.

When you reach intense orgasms in this manner, after a while there will come a shift in your consciousness. There is even a possibility that you may find satiety and gradually pursue chastity. But never force yourself out of your way. That's not how it works. You should seek pleasure wherever it is available to you, just know that a higher form is within reach, and it costs you nothing to obtain it."

"And what is that form?"

"Tranquility. When you're able to simply sit under a tree, contemplate nature, and marvel at its wonders; when boredom ceases to exist, and every minute of your being consists of perfect harmony and peace, for nothing is able to disturb you; then you will know that you have reached your destination, and have, in fact, become a god."

14

After a day packed with knowledge, we were given some leisure time to take a stroll around the countryside and enjoy the villa. We regrouped in the evening to drink wine around a bonfire. Everyone was really friendly, regardless of their age. I used to hold biases against old people, thinking them bitter and grumpy, but here, all the grandpas and grandmas were remarkably relaxed and not judgmental as I thought people their age tended to be. We told jokes, shared laughter, and had a fantastic time at the expense of the gods.

The following day, we convened once more with Diana and Artemius for a second lecture on their respective subjects. The agenda was steered towards practical and lighter content, not so heavy with theory, to ensure that we would have sufficient energy and focus for the evening session, which we were told would be "a treat." Various topic options were available to choose from, but once again, I opted for a men-only workshop that was going to focus on "how to achieve happiness with oneself."

It was a beautiful night, with a starry sky overhead. A gentle breeze added to the pleasure as we sat comfortably on the grass, eagerly awaiting our instructor. Taurus, a muscular man—who lived up to his name—greeted us warmly. He was clad in a thin loose tunic that allowed us to catch glimpses of his massive pectorals and arms as he moved. Three musicians carrying different instruments accompanied him.

"Welcome, my dear students. The initial objective of this session is to help you become more at ease with your own bodies. To start, I would like to ask you to remove your tunics; keep only your loincloths on."

The coolness of the night felt like a delicious wrap on my skin.

"I encourage you to take a moment to look around. As you can see, there are men of all shapes and forms here. I want you to refrain from passing any kind of judgment. We're here to partake in a special evening of friendship among males, and honor and respect each other accordingly."

I looked around me. Beside me were men of all ages, from youngsters to sexagenarians. I can't say I found any of them attractive, but I was committed to adhering to Taurus's guidance, concentrating on building camaraderie rather than stimulating any sexual instincts.

"This knowledge, has been handed down to us from the great cultures of the faraway land of Serica, through the masters and scribes of Greece. It can serve not only as a means of finding pleasure, but also to heal, for after all, the feeling of bodily well-being is one of the greatest pleasures there can be." He paced back and forth as he spoke. "Although this wisdom encompasses many components and stages, which we will gradually explore, it is based on one single concept: that orgasm and ejaculation are two different things."

I looked around to see the reactions. No one seemed to mind that the instructor was speaking so eruditely of tavern talk.

"If you believe that the ultimate pleasure in this world comes from allowing the vital fluid to leave your body, you're mistaken; but don't worry, so are most men." He paused briefly. "In this workshop, you'll acquire the techniques to experience not just one, but multiple orgasmic summits in a single pleasuring session, how to make those sensations course through your body, and above all, how to retain a portion of that pleasure throughout the day, without feeling drained or tired."

It all sounded fantastic, if a bit overly ambitious. What more could a man wish for?

He spoke a little about the ancient culture that had discovered these secrets some six hundred years ago, in a land that no Roman had ever set foot on. To give a time perspective, he joked that at that time, in this part of the world, Romulus and Remus were still being suckled by the she-wolf.

According to those wise men, this knowledge could not only lead to greater sexual satisfaction, but also contribute to overall well-being and longevity. These men were physicians who valued physical and spiritual wellness equally. In their culture, these aspects were not separate as they were for us in Rome; in fact, sexual satisfaction could be used as a means to achieve the other two objectives. This was not a religion but rather a system of knowledge.

Then he mentioned something that left me slightly disappointed: while he would unveil most of the secrets in this session, he emphasized that becoming a master required practice, and it would take several days, or even weeks, for us to fully experience the benefits in our own bodies. Today, he would just provide the basics. Nonetheless, he had my full attention.

He reiterated that the primary goal was to attain orgasm while retaining the seed, as it held the essential energy that, when skillfully channeled through the body via pleasurable sensations, had the potential to improve health, boost creativity and foster spiritual growth.

"Alright, my dear men, enough talk," he declared with a clap. "Let's get down to action."

He signaled to the musicians, who began playing a relaxing melody. At first, the harp played alone, accompanied by intermittent tambourine beats. An aulos player stood by their side but remained silent.

"The first thing we're going to work on is your breathing. I want you to close your eyes, sit with your legs crossed and your back straight, hands on your navel and shoulders relaxed. Now inhale through your nose, allowing your abdomen to expand. With your chest relaxed, I want you to exhale, letting your abdomen return to its original position. Understand?"

"Yes."

"Excellent. Now, let's practice. Inhale... exhale... inhale... exhale."

We did that about thirty times.

"I want you to breathe more deeply... Inhale... exhale... Ensure you utilize the full capacity of your stomach for expansion... Inhale... exhale... Focus on your genitalia and synchronize it with the rhythm... Inhale... exhale... Very good."

We continued for a few more minutes.

"Turn your attention now to your anus and your perineum. When you inhale, contract the muscles in that region, and relax them as you exhale. Inhale... exhale... If necessary, also contract your eyes and mouth to assist in contracting those muscles down there. Try different things until you find what works best for you, but make sure to engage them. Inhale... exhale..."

After a few minutes of practice, he said, "Here comes the interesting part. I want you to untie your *subligaculum* and expose your genitalia. Keep your eyes closed. Focus solely on yourself. Forget about your companions; they are no longer here. Even I am not present. I'm just a voice within your mind. In this moment, it's just you and nature... just you and the moon, the wind, the sky..."

The music changed to a more sensual tone, the aulos joining in with the sound.

"I want you to touch yourself... Something you've surely done before. If you need to evoke thoughts that make you feel aroused, feel free to do so. Bring to your mind anything that makes you aroused. There's no one to judge you… Here it's only you… and the music…"

Of course, I thought of Renatus, especially that first time I jerked him off until he cummed. However, since the goal here was not to ejaculate, I focused on how I teased him by withholding his pleasure. I recalled the scent of his skin and… the sweetness of his moans… I was hard in an instant.

"Follow the music… follow the sound…" Taurus's voice said—for it was now just a voice.

The music was a good guide to what we were trying to achieve. The rhythm told you when to speed up and when to slow down; when to get more intense and when to relax.

"Now I'm going to share with you three simple techniques that will be useful for you as beginners. The first one is pumping, which you should be familiar with, since it is what men normally do when they masturbate. It consists of running your curled hand up and down your shaft. Pumping is what you do when you want to extract the fluid quickly. Even if right now this is not your objective, you can use this technique to initiate the session or when you've become too relaxed and feel like you're losing your hard on and want to get back to a state of arousal promptly."

"The second technique is tapping. As the name implies, it consists of tapping your hard member when it's fully erect and you're close to reaching orgasm, and also when you're already feeling the tingling inside and want it to last longer, but without risking spilling the seed. This is the main fine control technique."

"The third technique is bending. Here, depending on the angle of your erection, you want to bend your erect cock down or sideways and let it spring back to its normal position. This fine control technique is a fun way to diversify the pleasure and, as long as it doesn't cause you pain, it can allow you to continue masturbating without increasing the intensity too much."

"Now, the idea here is that you use these three strokes— and others that you find pleasurable—as a combination that works to maximize your pleasure. Depending on your previous degree of arousal, just a few minutes of pumping can get you close to orgasm: slow down and try to stay in that state as long as possible using the two fine control techniques. It's good to even feel some tingling but avoid going overboard and spilling the seed."

He gave us a few minutes to try it out. After some time, I learned to identify when I was getting close and when I would normally cum if I kept going. So I stopped there. I tapped my penis or bent it, depending on how I felt. A slight, pleasant tingling appeared in an indetermined area inside my pelvis; I tried to hold it in as much as possible.

"Moving forward, I want you to learn one last technique today. If you're really close to orgasm, and you feel like you're about to cum, as a last resource you can try gripping your balls and cock, and also putting pressure on your perineum with your fingers. This technique has the potential to even stop the flow of sperm, but it's not totally effective. It's best if you don't reach the point of no return. But this can help if you do."

A man moaned beside me. "Ahh, ahh! Too late for me!"

"Too late for me too," another said.

"Alright," Taurus said with a chuckle. "This tells me that's enough for today. Open your eyes. You may rest now."

We opened our eyes and exchanged smiles. Some of the men cracked jokes.

"If you managed to get close to orgasm without spilling your seed, congratulations. If not, don't feel bad—this is only your first session. You'll have all the time in the world to master the techniques later on."

I was proud that I hadn't spilled my seed. Only a little precum had come out, but Taurus said it was normal. Some of the tingling remained inside me, making me relaxed and satisfied.

15

I slept better than I had in weeks. The previous night's session did not leave me tired, just extremely relaxed, and in the morning I woke up with a burst of energy. After a simple breakfast of bread and water, I joined what I was told would be a very important philosophical session. Diana greeted us as we gathered beneath a fig tree.

"Have you been enjoying the retreat so far, my dear ones?"

The participants responded with cheers.

"I'm hoping that at least you remember the two main conclusions we reached during our initial meeting. Can anyone tell me those?"

"That we should not fear the gods."

"That death is nothing to us."

"Very good, very good! It's great to see that even with the intense pleasures you've been experiencing, you haven't forgotten the most crucial aspects of the retreat."

The attendees laughed.

"Today I want to go deeper into those subjects. Let's go back again to the atoms," she said to exclamations of disappointment. "Yes, yes, my dear ones, I promise you it won't take long. You will soon find out why it is necessary."

She went on, refreshing our memory on the basics of the physics that govern the world.

"So," she said as a concluding remark, "as you've now learned, the atoms didn't enter into an agreement to come together and form the universe. The world and everything we know and see simply came into being without any purpose or plan. I think that's pretty well understood by now, am I right?"

We all nodded.

"Very well!" She smiled, clasping her hands. "Now I'm going to present the following scenario. Let's say that poor Artemius's..." she said, grinning at him, "...house is struck by lightning, causing it to catch fire. What do you consider to be the cause?"

The attendees reflected among themselves.

"Was it because he's a very sinful man and deserved to be punished?"

"No," some replied.

"Was it because he had offended the gods, and they decreed his misery?"

"No," more attendees replied.

"Was it because, although he is a good man, Jupiter dispatched his mighty thunderbolt merely to amuse himself?"

"No."

"Then what is the reason?"

There was silence.

"The evident reason is this: the atoms forming the clouds accumulated and friction between them led to their collision, causing the discharge of lightning. This means that it was a purely chance occurrence, something that could happen to anyone."

"Indeed, even statues of Jupiter are occasionally struck by lightning," a man said.

"Exactly. All natural phenomena are outcomes of the motion of innumerable atoms, and if we could track each and every one of them, we would even be able to forecast when and where lightning would strike. It's a matter of physics and not religion."

As strange as it sounded, I comprehended it clearly: there was no underlying reason for the catastrophe. From nature's perspective, it was not even a catastrophe, but a simple rearrangement of atoms. It was not a punishment for his sins, nor was it meant to teach him a lesson about the transience of life, or anything of the kind.

Despite the potential peril of this knowledge, it offered an extraordinary way to live without anxiety. However, it also meant living without the solace of religion and the comfort provided by—albeit ineffective—prayer. *The truth is that we're powerless in the face of such occurrences, whether we acknowledge it or not.*

"Now, let's consider some of the opposing viewpoints to our doctrine. Artemius, would you mind bringing up the first one?"

He stood up. "Plato asserts that the cosmos is a living entity with a soul. Therefore—he argues—if objects like stars and planets are integral parts of the cosmos, they too must be alive and have their own will, which is intrinsically connected with the will of the gods."

"Do you see the absurdity of this claim? Do fish live in the air? Does sap grow from rocks? No, right? Well, my friends, just as fish and sap cannot survive outside of their respective environments, neither can souls exist apart from living beings: clods of earth, balls of fire, and seas of water cannot possess minds because they don't have the conditions to do so. On to the next argument."

"Some Eastern sects," Artemius continued, "claim that the world was created by an omnipotent, omniscient, and omnibenevolent god, and therefore it has a purpose and operates according to his commands."

"This is a vicious field. In response to these religious fanatics, the Epicurean teachers have put forward the following argument: If such a god desires to eradicate evil but is unable to do so, then he is not omnipotent; if he is capable but chooses not to, he is malevolent; if he possesses both the power and the will to eliminate evil, why does evil still exist?; and lastly, if he lacks both the ability and the will to do so, why call him god?"

His words gave me an inner jolt. How could anyone counter such an argument?

"These people will come back and spit sophisms at you," Diana continued, "but I can tell you one thing: no one can prove this proposition wrong. We know that it did not originate from the master himself, for he did not live in the same era as these hypocrites. However, his followers are an enlightened sort, and they have continued to protect the truth with their intellect after the master's demise."

"Does this mean that the gods don't exist at all?" I dared to ask.

"As you may recall, dear, we Epicureans neither affirm nor deny the existence of the many gods of the people. We merely state that if the gods do exist, they are entirely oblivious to human suffering or happiness; they live in a state of bliss that we should endeavor to attain for ourselves. The philosophical problem mentioned earlier concerns the existence of an all-powerful, all-knowing, and all-good deity, which we can confidently assure does not exist. And this leads us to the next point. Artemius, would you care to explain it?"

"Of course. I believe we can all conclude now that the world we inhabit was not created for our benefit: much of the world is inhospitable to human life; it is difficult to grow the crops we need to survive; natural disasters frequently devast our cities; wild animals are looking to devour us, and dreadful diseases plague us. There is no god, whether above or below, responsible for all these occurrences. They are simply aspects of the mechanics and randomness of the world. All we can do is strive to comprehend the conditions that lead to these events, so that we can continue to advance our civilization despite of a world that is alien to us."

"To conclude," Diana said, "we're here on our own, and we must face the world with that mindset. We should worry only about what's in our hands. Of course, I say 'worry' only as a figure of speech, as we must live free of worry and anxiety, and the best way to do it is in the company of friends. Therefore, if you haven't already done so, I encourage you to get to know your fellow participants and enjoy the benefits of one of the greatest boons in this world: friendship."

I went for a walk alone on the beach. I needed some time to meditate on what I had been listening to. I felt better but was still not totally at peace. Occasionally, thoughts of my captivity made my body shudder. The retreat had been wonderful so far; I only wished Renatus was with me. *He's all I need to feel complete.*

A cool breeze surprised me, and I wrapped my arms around myself. As I was heading back to the villa, I spotted a young man standing by the beach, tossing stones into the sea.

"That one didn't go very far."

He turned to look at me. "Yeah, I know. Just like me."

"What do you mean?"

"I'm not sure. That's just how I feel."

"Why are you here?"

"My parents sent me. You know, wealthy Greek folks from Pompeii, looking to get rid of their son for a while as they enjoy social gatherings and dice games."

"I'm amazed that they even allow you get in contact with these ideas. Are they Epicureans? My parents would never let me. They'd consider these people dangerous and subversive. I'm Lucius from Neapolis, by the way," I said, offering a handshake.

"I'm Basileus," he said, shaking my hand. "No, they're not really Epicureans. They sympathize with some of the ideas but would never give up their wealth for a life of simplicity." He paused, looking at the sea. After a while, he redirected his gaze at me. "Why are you here?"

"It's a long story. I'm recovering from… trauma." I briefly recounted my experience with the kidnapping.

"I'm sorry to hear that, *amice*. Yeah, those baths can be dangerous. I never go to any other but the Stabians with friends or my parents."

We lapsed into silence, gazing at the waves crashing on the shore. I glanced at him discreetly. His skin was tanned—nearly as much as Renatus's—and he had a prominent moon mark on his upper arm. He was kind of cute, with short curly hair and a little nose, but my heart was already occupied. Moreover, I didn't know if he was into men. However, his serene demeanor gave me courage to share a bit more about myself.

"I also have another issue…"

"What is it?" he asked, looking at me.

"That I… prefer the company of men, if you know what I mean."

He returned his attention to the sea, tossing another stone. "I don't see the big deal about it." He looked back at me. "I'm into women, but your preference doesn't make me uncomfortable."

"Thank you." I lowered my gaze.

"Don't be ashamed of it. Some men are into women, some into other men. It shouldn't be a problem."

"For some people it is."

"For your parents?"

I nodded. "Especially my father. I don't think my mother would care much, but she does everything he tells her to."

"Do they know about you?"

"I don't know. I don't think so. Well... maybe they have suspicions. Every parent knows their child."

"Not necessarily. Some parents, particularly fathers, don't bother to get to know their children very much."

"Maybe that's the situation with my father. I don't think he ever cared much about me. He just wants me to perpetrate the family name, to live up to the life he's planned for me, without considering my thoughts or feelings."

I gave him a hug.

"It's alright, *amice*," he said, patting me on the back. "That's why you're here, to heal."

"That's true," I said letting go of him.

"By the way, do you know what tonight's session with Taurus will be about?"

"No idea, but last one was fun, wasn't it?"

"Yeah, it's the best part of this retreat. I don't really care for the 'philosophy' much, but these self-pleasuring techniques are awesome. I heard that for tonight's session, we will need a partner. Would you like to team up with me?"

"Of course! I'm glad you asked. I wouldn't have wanted to partner with one of those old folks. Nothing against them, but it was a man their age who attacked me."

"I get it. No worries, I'll help you heal!" A gust of wind swept over us. "Let's go back to the villa; it's getting a bit cold here."

16

We met for the second session with Taurus, this time in a carpeted room amid the sweet fragrance of burning incense sticks, as the evening had become too chilly for comfort.

"*Salvete*, my dear trainees," Taurus greeted us. "Tonight, I have a very special session for you, which will require you to pair up. Take a look around and find a partner for the night. And remember that physical appearances don't matter for these methods."

I smiled at Basileus and reached for his hand. Taurus's assistants provided candles to each couple, positioning them on either side.

"To start, disrobe completely and sit cross-legged, facing your partner. The aim of these exercises is to bring the mind and body into balance by increasing your sexual energy."

I glanced at Basileus, and we exchanged smiles. We were ready.

"First, place your hand over your partner's heart, and have him do the same. Start breathing deeply, experiencing each other's energy, and concentrating on your partner's heartbeat. Maintain eye contact; it's very important to build intimacy."

A harp and an aulos played softly in the background.

"Synchronize your breathing. Visualize yourselves as one as you feel the air coursing through you. The energy we are going to generate today will be twice as potent as what you could produce individually, so there's a synergistic element that you will benefit from."

We continued the exercise for a while longer.

"If you find this monotonous or feel that nothing is really happening, take more time to internalize your partner's breathing, to sense that it merges seamlessly with your own."

I didn't find it boring at all; I was indeed experiencing a deep, emotional connection with Basileus.

"Now I want one of you to sit on your partner's thighs, wrap your legs around his back, put your arms around him, and touch foreheads. Continue focusing on each other's breathing and heartbeat."

I took the initiative and sat on his lap, following Taurus's instructions.

"At this stage, you can either maintain eye contact with your partner or close your eyes, whichever feels more comfortable."

We instinctively closed our eyes.

"Feel the energy accumulating in your pelvic area and the arousal it provokes."

That was true. My rod had already become steel.

"Now, let your penis rest on your partner's penis. This will serve as the primary connection point for the exchange of energy."

I maneuvered my hard cock closer to Basileus's until they were in full vertical contact. An exquisite weightiness drew them together, akin to magnets—no doubt the energy Taurus was speaking of.

"Now, concentrate on letting that energy travel through your bodies. It will flow in a circle; you'll sense it ascending your spine to your forehead, then disappearing—which is when it traverses through your partner's body—before returning to your own body through the point of contact below, which is your penis." He paused. "Don't rush; take your time. And don't worry if it doesn't come immediately."

At first I didn't feel much—just the energy building up in my pelvic area—but soon, a slight tingling sensation ran through my body like a shooting star.

"Embrace a little closer if you feel like it; caress your partner's back, brush cheeks, lock lips if you want to… Move in a rocking motion, but slowly…"

We moved as if we were making love, except it was our cocks sliding on each other. My balls were fully charged; a spark would fly if I touched them.

"Open yourselves to your inner light by keeping your eyes closed. Let go of your thoughts and feel the energy that now flows through your bodies like a river. Surrender to your desires and deepen the intimacy between the two of you by touching noses and sharing the same breath."

The intensity of our arousal and the pleasure of the activity heightened.

"You are gods who have discovered each other in a journey through this world. This is the bliss felt by the Olympians, and it should be the purpose of your earthly existence... Pleasure, and nothing but pleasure..."

"The time has come to make things a little more intense, my friends. I want you to practice the cock exercises I taught you last time, but with your partner's cock. Next to you, you will find jars of warm scented oil."

I poured some oil on my palm and reached down to touch his cock and stroke it gently. He did the same with mine. I slid his foreskin up and down the glans, using the oil to provide additional lubrication to the precum.

"There are several new moves you can try. For example, cupping the head of your partner's cock with your fingers, making sure the foreskin slides up and down and provides a pleasurable rubbing."

"You can also place your open hand on one side of his cock, and the other open hand on the other side, like two walls enclosing the divine rod. Slide your hands in opposite directions to stimulate the member."

"Or hold the cock with one hand, keeping the foreskin down, and provide a massage with your other hand, moving it in circles over the glans. The stimulation will be very intense, so be careful. From time to time, stroke your partner's body to help spread the energy. As the receiver, give yourself up to the rising surges of energy that will flood your body."

We added some moves of our own and stroked each other's abdomens, chests, and legs. An intense heat took over my body.

"One of you take the two cocks together with one hand, applying gentle pressure. Rub the phalluses up and down, letting them feel each other along the shaft and dance with each other, akin to kindling a fire.

I stroked our cocks together starting at the base, working my way up to the heads, varying the speed and pressure, letting our glandes touch and wet each other, mixing our precum.

"You can do this for as long as you like, until you start feeling the tingle of orgasm again, at which point you should stop pleasuring your partner and take control of your own cock, since only you can feel how close you are to ecstasy."

This happened after a while. I tapped Basileus on the arm to let him know I was close. We kept touching each other's bodies with one hand and stroking our own cocks with the other. A wound was opening inside me, causing pleasure rather than pain. I focused on breathing, the gentle sensation of Basileus's skin, and the unfettered flow of energy coursing through our bodies. I signaled Basileus to stop or I would cum soon.

At night, I was still very sexually energized and felt like playing with myself some more, now in the privacy of my room. I had discovered many secrets about my body in a very short time, and my curiosity had been ignited. Taurus had emphasized the significance of preserving one's seed, so I would be careful not to spill it if I was going to aim for another summit.

I lay naked on the bed and began the stimulation; it didn't take me long to reach a full erection. Then I practiced all the new strokes I had learned; I pumped my cock, tapped it when I had gotten close, and bent and released it to prolong the tingle of the impending orgasm. I massaged my balls when I wanted to relax a bit.

I used Taurus's technique to move the energy through the body: squeezing one's buttocks and using them to pump it upward. I did this for a few minutes, breathing deeply to help the flow. A strong inner energy warmed my pelvic area and moved slowly up my spine. *It is happening.* I kept pumping with my buttocks more and more until the magic appeared.

The divine energy reached my head and burst in the most intense pleasure sensation I had ever felt. Stars swirled in frantic motion inside my head. My breathing intensified and a wonderful feeling stirred in my racing heart. Every inch of my being was vibrating in tune with the universe. In me there was only forgiveness and peace; all I could feel was love for my fellow men. I was convinced that I had been somehow elevated to the celestial realms. The sensation Taurus had described was undeniably real. I touched my cock and noticed I had not expelled a single drop of my seed. My balls still felt full, but I wasn't anxious. I was at peace.

17

The day following that transformative experience it was time to return to Pompeii. I bid farewell to my new friends—especially Basileus—promising we would meet again. The family who had taken me to Herculaneum arrived to pick me up once more, and they dropped me off at Eusebius's *domus*, apologizing for not having the time to stay for a chat. Overjoyed at the prospect of reuniting with my adoptive kin, I was determined to make amends for my discourtesy and bring them joy in any way I could. My affection for them had doubled and I felt like a fool for ever harboring uncertainties about their intentions.

I rapped on the door with a smile on my face but was greeted only by silence. Strange, since it was not locked from the outside. Knocking forcefully once more and receiving no response, I pushed the door open. A sense of foreboding gripped my heart as I walked through the abandonment that reigned in the house. I called out their names, but my voice echoed unanswered. Terrified, I rushed back outside.

"Young man, how good of you to come." A woman, one of the neighbors, approached me.

"What happened?" I asked in a trembling voice.

"Something terrible. Several men from the *pervigilia* came and took them away!"

"When?"

"Three days ago. We asked the officials where they were taking them, but they refused to give any explanation."

I thanked the distraught woman and ran to the city magistrate's office in the Temple of Saturn—the only place I could think of where I might find any clues.

A guard halted me at the entrance. "What's your business?"

"There's an important question I need to ask a magistrate."

"Which magistrate?"

"Ehm… Publius Maximus."

"There's no magistrate by that name here."

"Officer, please, I really need to talk to someone in this building."

He stood firm by the door, unwilling to speak or meet my gaze. I walked away, disheartened. Then I thought of another possibility: the *custodia publica*. They had to be there, or at least someone there should know their whereabouts. I sprinted and after a few minutes arrived at the poorly maintained building.

"I'm here for a family visit," I said to the guard.

"Do you have an appointment?"

"No, but—"

"You need an appointment. Book it and come back on the date they tell you."

"Where?"

"In the Temple of Saturn."

I stood there momentarily, frustrated, but then my mood shifted. Armed with a specific request, that guard couldn't prevent me from entering now. I walked back to the temple, where the ill-tempered man was still standing in the doorway.

"You again?"

"I need to make an appointment for a visit to the *custodia publica*."

"There," he said, pointing to a small door in an adjacent building.

A daunting line of people waited outside. I positioned myself at the end. An hour later, an elderly woman finally assisted me.

"I need an appointment for a family visit to the *custodia publica*."

"What's the inmate's name?"

"Actually it's three people. Eusebius Calventius, his wife Gaia, and their son, Renatus."

She wrote the names on a small piece of papyrus and affixed a wax seal. I looked at the date in disbelief—thirty days later.

"What? No, you don't understand, I need to see them today."

She looked at me with impatience. "Appointments start next month."

"I understand, but—"

"You want it or not?"

I lowered my head and left.

That night, lying on my bed in Eusebius's *domus*, with a flickering candle on the bedside table, I pondered potential ways for infiltrating the prison. Slowly and methodically, I devised a plan. *Yes, this might work.* Feeling encouraged, I blew out the candle, aiming for a few hours of sleep. The anticipation of the impending mission mingled with the hope that gave solace to my restless mind.

At the first crow of the rooster, I walked to the *custodia publica* and stood hidden in an adjacent alley as the rising sun cast long shadows over the cobblestone streets and the ominous structure that imprisoned my friends.

I spent the day meticulously observing the guards' routine, committing to memory their movements and habits, and closely monitoring those who entered and exited. As the daylight slowly waned, a boy arrived with a donkey carrying two amphorae.

"Dinner is here!" he announced. The guards permitted him entry without question.

I waited for him to leave and observed as the guard who had previously denied me access was replaced by another. A few minutes later, the food courier came out of the prison and loaded the empty amphorae onto his donkey. I followed him.

The next afternoon, I stationed myself at the *thermopolium* where he had left the donkey, keeping a lookout for him. He appeared at sunset.

"Hey, where are you taking that food?"

"It's none of your business."

"Listen, we have unexpected guests at home, so we're needing some extra food. Do you think you could sell it to me? All the *thermopolia* are now closed."

"It's already paid for."

"Then you can make twice the money," I said, pulling out a small purse.

"Talk to my master then, I can't sell this without permission."

I opened the purse and let the coins glint in the fading sunlight.

The boy glanced nervously at both sides of the street. "This is for the *custodia publica* and they'll complain to my master if the food doesn't arrive."

"Then give some of this money to your master and keep the rest for yourself." His hesitation indicated my victory. "Besides, do you really think the guards care if the inmates eat?"

"No, but—"

"Take it." I pressed the bag firmly into his hand. "Your master will thank you and come up with an excuse."

He glanced around again and accepted the money. "But you can't use the donkey."

The amphorae turned out to be heavier than I had anticipated; I had to stop at every block to give my hands a rest, but I walked with determination. Upon reaching the prison, I hid behind a corner and verified that the guard had changed.

"Dinner has arrived," I announced in my best merchant tone.

"Why so late?" the guard asked. "And where's the donkey?"

"My master had to use it for another task today."

He eyed me suspiciously. "I hadn't seen you before. Are you from the 'Gustus Romanus' *thermopolium*?"

I nodded.

He motioned for me to come in.

Inside, the dimly lit room revealed the guards immersed in a game of dice. The rhythmic clatter of the cubes resonated through the air and a heavy stench of wine lingered, evidence of the indulgence that accompanied their leisure. The flickering light of a small lantern cast shadows on the walls, creating an atmosphere of clandestine revelry.

"We were beginning to think you were going to let the prisoners starve," one of the guards said.

"I doubt they'll miss that shit," another guard chimed in, eliciting laughter from his companions.

"I apologize. My master ran into some trouble. He—"

"Save your breath," the first guard said, getting up to open an iron door. "You know what to do, right? Or should I accompany you?"

"No need."

As soon as I entered, the inmates held out their hands with their plates, rattling them against the cold iron bars. The dim light accentuated the despair etched on their faces as they hurled a chorus of curses at me for the delay. "I'm hungry! This had better not be spoiled like last time.

143

I recoiled at the noxious odor and the wretched state of the surroundings. *Renatus's family is going through all this misery—just because of me.*

I moved from one cell to the next, pouring the repugnant concoction onto the inmates' plates. With each step, my heart pounded at the prospect of encountering my cherished family in the next cell. Disappointment had already taken hold of me when I reached the last division of the row, but a mixture of joy and sadness enveloped me when I peeked inside and discovered Eusebius and Gaia sitting on a bench.

"Eusebius! Gaia!" I hissed.

"Lucius!" the old man exclaimed, hastening toward the barred door, Gaia rushing alongside him.

"Oh dear, how wonderful it is to see you," she said, clasping my hands.

"How could you get in?" Eusebius asked.

"It doesn't matter. By the heavens, why did they bring you here?"

"We've been accused of defaulting on our land taxes for the last ten years," he replied. "But it's all a mistake. Our payments are in order, despite the magistrate's assertion that there's no record of them in the city archives. Luckily, we maintain our own *tabulārium*. Some friends are gathering all the necessary evidence to present before the *iudices* and clarify the situation. Don't worry at all, Lucius. We'll be out of here soon."

"But where is Renatus?" I peered into the cell. "Why isn't he here with you?"

"We don't know where they've taken him," Gaia replied, her eyes filled with tears. My heart ached to see her so distraught. "Lucius, please help us find out where he is and whether he is——"

"Ask no more. I know where to look. Rest assured that this will all be resolved very soon," I said, firmly holding her hands. "I can't stay long. I came with the excuse of bringing food to the inmates." Glancing around cautiously, I handed them two loaves of bread I had concealed inside my tunic. "At least you can dip these in the *puls*."

"Oh, thank you, dear Lucius!" Gaia said.

The relief I had felt at finding them was incomplete. My heart ached with a pain I had never known before. Renatus, where was he?

Book Four

18

When I arrived at my house in Neapolis the next day, sometime past *meridies*, everything felt cold and distant—no longer like home. I walked past the potted plants in the *impluvium*, the brightly colored frescoes in the atrium that my father took so much pride in, and the green curtains leading to the garden, and headed toward my mother's *solarium*. The door was ajar. She knitted a stola, in her usual contemplative calm, as delicate rays of sunlight touched her face. She seemed a bit older than when I last saw her a few months ago; in fact, this was the first time I noticed some strands of gray in her ladylike hairdo.

Without knocking, I carefully opened the door. She turned her face toward me and gasped.

"Lucius, by Juno! Thank the heavens you're here." She rushed to embrace me. "I've prayed so hard for you to come back."

"I didn't come back to stay, Mother. At least, not in the same way. Is Father here?"

She shook her head. "He'll be home soon. Please, have a seat," she showed me to a divan. "Why did you leave like that, Son?"

"I thought you would have figured it out by now." I paused, gazing into her eyes. "I'm afraid of Father."

"I know your father can be difficult at times, but running away is not the solution, Lucius. You've already worn the *toga virilis*, and it's only a matter of time before you will marry."

"That's precisely the problem," I said, rising to my feet. "Married life is not for me."

"Nonsense. You are a man now and you must start acting like one. Every man has a family, a job, and duties to attend to. And your father has planned such a great future for you…"

"But what if I have other plans? What if—"

"You must be tired, honey. Have you eaten yet? Why don't we go to the *triclinium*? I can have something light to keep you company."

I was definitely hungry, so I did not object. My mother instructed Martia, the old slave woman who had cared for me since my childhood, to bring me *prandium*. She greeted me solemnly, yet I could see the joy in her eyes.

We were dining quietly when the noise of the street door opening and approaching footsteps reached us.

"That's him." My mother dabbed her lips with a napkin and quickly stood up. "I'll go inform him of your presence, so he won't be caught by surprise."

The imposing man, clad in his customary pristine white toga, stepped into the *triclinium* before she could reach the door.

He looked at me with a deadpan expression. "I'll be in the *tablinum*," he said to my mother.

"Don't you want to talk to your son?" I overheard her asking him in the hallway.

Some time passed, during which I finished my meal. I needed a full stomach to confront the man.

"Go and see your father now," my mother said upon returning, her face etched with worry.

"Did he mention that he wants to talk to me?"

"No, but that's what you should do."

My father was sitting at his desk, engrossed in the perusal of documents. I positioned myself directly in front of him, denying him the possibility of ignoring me.

"I need a word with you," I said in the firmest tone I could muster.

"Later," he replied without glancing up. "I'm busy with matters that require immediate attention."

"There are other matters that require immediate attention too, Father." I said, seizing the scrolls he was examining. "You must order the release of Eusebius and Gaia!"

He finally directed the gaze of his intense green eyes to me. "I don't know what you're talking about."

"Yes you do," I said, pounding the table. "Order their release immediately!" My heart was beating fast. I had never dared to raise my voice to my father before.

"Don't yell at me, young man. You may be of age, but this is still my *domus*. I don't know what you've picked up in the company of those individuals, but I won't tolerate bad manners here."

"You will tolerate more than bad manners," I said, pushing the papyri off the desk. "And I insist that you order their release immediately."

"Or what?"

"You've underestimated them. Eusebius is a reputable man. He has proof that he has dutifully paid his taxes all these years. It's only a matter of time before the charges are cleared and they go free, and you'll end up looking like a fool. You can still avoid your embarrassment if you are the one who orders their release."

"You don't simply enter my *tablinum* and dictate what I should do."

"Well, I'm here now. Isn't that what you wanted?"

"Not everything."

"What else do you want, then?"

"I want you to make me proud, acting like my son." He stood up. "I want you to marry and pursue a career in law, like me."

"I don't want to do that," I said, tugging at my hair. "I've told you multiple times that I don't want to marry and that I have no desire to study law either."

"Then what do you want to do? You lack the physique to be an athlete, and the foxiness to be a merchant."

"I want to be an artist."

"An artist?" He laughed. His guffaw was so thunderous that my mother came to see what was happening. "Did you hear that, Pomponia? Your son wants to be an artist!"

"Why don't you listen to him, Successianus? Perhaps there's a way to find a compromise."

"There's no room for compromise in this discussion," he bellowed. "Lucius will do as I say, when I say. And the only way for him to free his friends is to agree to marry a lady of my choosing."

"Did you hear anything I said? They're working on their release right now. You can't use that to coerce me."

"There's something else I can do."

I looked at him in terror, anticipating what his next words would entail.

"Unless you comply with my orders, you'll never see that boy ever again."

"What did you do to him? He's not guilty of anything."

"He's guilty of turning you against us." He gripped my arms. "Now it's time for you to speak up. How long have you known him?"

I stepped away. "I met him the day after I ran away."

"I don't believe it."

"Why don't you believe it?"

"You had already been seeing him behind my back, hadn't you? Long before you ran away."

"You have no base for what you're saying, Father. They're from Pompeii; I'd never been there before. How could I have met him?"

"You have a lot to explain to me. You will sit here and tell me precisely how things unfolded."

I obeyed. My mother stood behind me, placing her hands on my shoulders. I fed him the details, starting from with my escape from the pomegranate picker, the encounter with the wolf, to my time at Eusebius's farm. Naturally, I omitted any reference to the sentimental situation between Renatus and me. Still, I was frightened by the piercing look my father would cast at me from time to time, as if he somehow intuited the true nature of our relationship.

"And why were you in Pompeii?"

"They took me there when your men were searching for me."

"Then they're your accomplices. They should have handed you over."

"I begged them not to."

"Why do they care so much about you? You're nothing but a foolish child."

"Because, unlike you, they're good people with noble feelings."

"Why weren't you at their home when they were arrested?"

"They had sent me to a retreat home in Herculaneum."

He frowned, eyeing me with disbelief. "Herculaneum? That city is even more sinful than Pompeii. It's the seat of those atheists who are ruining the empire with their preaching against the gods. Don't tell me," he said, spitting as he spoke, "that you took part in one of those sacrilegious ceremonies in which—"

"Don't worry, Father. I was simply taken to a serene countryside villa to reflect and regain my well-being. Nothing of the kind happened there." *If he only knew.* "That's all," I said, rising to my feet. "They're innocent and had nothing to do with me running away. They didn't even know who I was then, by Mercury! All they have done is help me. You should be grateful to them."

My father stood silently for a while, giving me hope that he might abandon his intentions.

"Very well, I will have them released."

"Thank you, Father."

"And as for your friend, you will see him again once your marriage to Laetitia Caecilia is finalized."

19

I pleaded with my parents for a modest wedding, but of course, they announced it to the four winds and made sure that the most important patrician families were invited.

The ceremony was held in my father-in-law's *domus*, one of the most opulent in all of Neapolis. The entrance was draped with festive tapestries and fabrics from the eastern part of the empire, a luxury that not many could afford. The wedding area in the atrium was adorned with a canopy of exotic flowers, and beautiful garlands embellished walls, doors, and columns.

Laetitia Caecilia was a strikingly beautiful young lady—only seventeen—with delicate ivory skin and long black curls framing her face gracefully. I didn't meet her until the ceremony, and immediately felt sorry for the unfortunate circumstances. She surely hoped to raise a conventional family with many children, unaware that I would never be able to give her what any man would strive to offer.

After pronouncing the vows, we stood in the atrium, accepting well wishes from the guests, some of which seemed genuine, although it was evident that some people resented the power our families would gain from this union.

I was lucky not only that my bride was beautiful and had a gracious demeanor, but that she really seemed like a good person. Yet, I was fully aware that the only reason he chose her was that Caecilia's father was the leader of a Senate faction with which my father had long wanted to align himself.

As the music commenced, I excused myself, leaving Caecilia alone at the main table, and went to find my father. He was holding a goblet of wine and was engaged in a conversation.

"Father, I need to talk to you," I said, taking him by the arm.

"Not now, Lucius."

"Right now." Earning peculiar looks from his colleagues, I unceremoniously pulled him away from the group and guided him to a balcony, away from prying eyes.

"Alright." His face showed an irritated expression. "What do you need?"

"I did what you asked me to do. Now tell me where Renatus is."

"You haven't consummated the marriage yet," he said, taking a sip of his wine.

"Where is he?" I clutched his toga, nearly causing him to spill his drink. "You will tell me this instant!"

"Don't make a scene." He placed his drink on the balustrade, looked around, and then turned his gaze back to me. "Well, Son, it's best you know the truth. I had requested a slave trader I occasionally work with to hold him for a while, hoping you'd come to your senses."

I stared at him with wild eyes.

"I spoke to him yesterday, mentioning that you were nearing your promise and to prepare to release him, but he informed me that he was made a very tempting offer, and…"

"And what?"

"He sold him to a foreign buyer. Greek, Egyptian… I can't recall. The fact is that your friend is gone, and there's nothing I can do now. I'm sorry."

I attempted to strike him, but he caught my fist.

"This is not the time to act like a little brat, Lucius. Look at your bride, how beautiful she is. You can't say I didn't choose well for you. You should be grateful. Not all the maidens in Rome are so gracious."

"Liar! You're a filthy liar!" I shouted, drawing the attention of several guests.

"Don't worry," he addressed them loudly. "My son is upset because he thinks the wedding isn't lavish enough. What do you make of that, folks?"

The guests chuckled and exchanged comments. My heart seethed with anger and despair. I wanted to shove him off the balcony. I lunged at him, but he caught my wrists.

"Don't turn this into a spectacle, Lucius. Look around. Do you want your bride's family to think you are a petulant child?"

"Why did you do this to me, Father? Why?" Tears welled in my eyes. I wanted to leap from the height myself.

"Someday, you'll thank me for saving your life. I know that some boys go through 'peculiar' phases growing up. You had developed a special affection for that boy, hadn't you?" His gaze pierced my thoughts. "You don't need to say it. I know. I saw it in your eyes when we talked about him. It's best for everyone that you and he are now apart."

I attempted to maintain eye contact, but my gaze fell downward. My entire body trembled.

"I'm certain you can still redirect your affections toward women. It shouldn't take much. Especially with a beautiful woman like your wife," he said, smiling and patting my face. "Relax, young man. Consider tonight. Let go of your old feelings for that boy and enjoy your wife. You have total freedom to do with her as you like. Women are... like property."

"Shut up! I don't want to hear any more."

My mother approached, wearing a deeply distressed expression. "Darling, it's time for you to take your bride home," she said, taking me by the hand. "The driver knows the way to your new *domus*, which your father has purchased for you. When you get off the coach, you'll have to carry her into the bedroom—"

"I know all that, Mother, you don't have to say it. You don't have to say anything," I said, walking away.

Cecilia and I remained silent during the downhill ride in the bridal carriage to the center of Neapolis. . What should have been an enjoyable experience for her turned into an ordeal due to the state of mind I was in. She might have assumed I was nervous, and I'm certain she was too, but whatever weighed on her mind, she honored my silence. We didn't even hold hands.

As the moment arrived, I carried her into our new *domus*, whose doors were opened by the carriage driver. He handed me the keys and extended his congratulations. The residence had already been decorated—to my father's taste—and a trail of rose petals led the way to our *cubiculum*. I laid her gently on one side of the bed and I sat on the other.

"What's wrong," she said in a soft, almost ethereal voice. "Am I so unattractive that you regret marrying me?"

"No, not at all," I said, looking at her. "How could you even say that? You're the most beautiful woman I've ever seen. This has nothing to do with you. It's just—"

"Don't be afraid," she said, taking my hand. "I don't know what you're supposed to do either. So… you've never been with a woman before?"

I shook my head. *Poor thing still thinks it's just nerves…*

"Then there's nothing to worry about. I guess we just have to let our instincts guide us and let nature do the rest…"

That was precisely the problem. Nature wouldn't act on me as it would on any other man, who by now would surely have a steely hard-on.

I lay down beside her, looking up at the ceiling, which featured a fresco of four putti playing trumpets among clouds. She leaned against me, resting on my arm. I turned to look at her. Witnessing her there, so innocent, so delicate, led me to tears.

"Oh no, husband, don't cry," she said, embracing me. "Please tell me what's wrong. We can't do anything tonight if you don't tell me... We are to live our life together, we need to start off the right way, trusting each other."

"Can I trust you?"

"Of course, I'm your wife."

"I... I'm not what you think," I said, looking into her eyes.

She gazed at me, perplexed.

"I don't like women the way other men do." My spine shivered as I uttered those words. *Now she'll run to her mother and tell her she had married an invert.*

She hugged me close, refusing to let go.

"I'm sorry. I'm so sorry, Caecilia. I didn't want to do this to you. This is my father's scheme. He tricked me into getting married."

She loosened up a bit and looked me straight in the eyes. "Now you need to tell me exactly what happened."

I told her how my father had relentlessly pressured me for months to take a wife, and how I had run away from home, met a boy, and fallen in love. I shared that I couldn't imagine life without him. I explained how my father had found out everything, kidnapped him, and forced me to marry her to secure his release. Finally, I disclosed his deceit, revealing that he had already sold him into slavery.

"By all the gods, your father is a monster!"

"That's an understatement. And I'm sorry he put you in the middle of all this. He hates women, he thinks of them as no more than furniture. I don't think he even loves my mother."

"Don't feel sorry for me. I feel sorry for you. And for your friend too. How could your father be so cruel?"

"You have no idea what he's capable of, out of greed and ambition."

She was silent for a minute. Then she said in a reassuring voice, "Don't worry, Lucius. I will help you."

I looked at her, astonished.

"I think it's best to pretend we're a couple for now. You know, play the game. That will give us time to find Renatus."

"Do you think we can still find him?"

"There might be a chance. And I'm sure you won't give up without trying."

"Of course, I won't. I'll go to the end of the world to find him!"

"And I'll go with you as your wife. Together, we are stronger," she said with a smile. "My family has an entourage of slaves and connections to traders. We can start from there."

"You divine creature." I leaned toward her and planted a kiss on her cheek.

"I thought you didn't like kissing girls," she said with a grin.

"Only as a brother," I said, winking.

I felt a glimmer of hope at last. I lay sideways on the bed, resting my arm on her stomach. Suddenly, I jolted upright, startled. "Don't they have to inspect the sheets tomorrow morning to see if… the marriage was consummated?"

"Yes," she hissed.

She got up and went to the kitchen, returning with a knife.

"What are you doing?" I said in terror.

"I'll just cut myself a little bit, so they'll think that—"

"You won't do such a thing," I said, jumping off the bed. I snatched the knife out of her hands. "I'll cut myself. I'm the one who put you in all this trouble."

"Let's do it early in the morning, then. We're both tired. Let's get some sleep, we have a lot of plans to carry out."

Happy, I gave her another brotherly kiss and curled up on my side of the bed.

20

"Lucius, wake up." Caecilia's voice reached me as I felt a gentle slap on my face.

Startled, I opened my eyes, needing a moment to reorient myself to reality. Sunlight streamed in through the window, and I found myself lying in bed next to Caecilia, drenched in sweat.

"What were those words you were saying?"

"What words?" I mumbled, sitting up slightly. "I have the most terrible headache."

"'What's good is easily attainable... what's dreadful is easily endured...' You were repeating those words endlessly. I was hesitant to wake you up, but you seemed increasingly agitated."

"Those words comprise half of the master's remedy for attaining tranquility. But if you say I was agitated, I guess they weren't having the intended effect on me."

"What is the other half?"

"Don't fear the gods. Don't worry about death."

She gave me a weird look. "Not fearing the gods? Not worrying about death? I've never heard such nonsense."

"The gods are indifferent to our existence, our suffering, or our joy," I said proudly, like a child repeating his lesson after school. "If they do exist, they reside in a state of eternal bliss, far removed from us but," I caught myself echoing Gaia's words, "I'm more inclined to believe they don't exist at all."

"Don't be horrid," she said, frowning. "They certainly do exist."

I didn't want to upset her with an argument. "Regardless, it's not death what I fear, but life. And it's not by praying that we're going to find Renatus. We must act."

"Thats true," she said, quickly getting out of bed. "Get ready. We have a lot of work to do."

We visited her parents early the next day. I reaffirmed the impression I had gained since the wedding ceremony—that they were good people, a truly noble family. While it was evident that Caecilia's father possessed wealth and wielded influence in the Senate and among merchants, he also exhibited high moral character. Her mother, too, was a moral woman who genuinely cared for others, including me. My parents could learn a lot from them.

"*Salvete, salvete*," her mother said with a beaming smile. "How are the newlyweds? We're so happy to see you." She warmly embraced us and called out instructions to the slaves to prepare hot milk with honey and sweetened bread for everyone.

Her father arrived and shook my hand. "Follow me, young man. I need to have a quick word with you."

165

I froze. *The last thing I need is more problems.*

Before he and I entered his *tablinum*, I overheard Caecilia's mother asking: "So how did everything go last night?" and Caecilia replying: "Wonderful. Nothing to complain about, Mother."

"Good," her mother said as they walked into the kitchen.

In the *tablinum*, Caecilia's father gestured for us to have a seat.

"So... no problems last night?"

I frowned. "No... no problems."

"You know what I mean, don't you?"

The intensity of his stare made me very uneasy.

"Of course, and I can assure you that there was no problem at all."

"So you... consummated the act?"

"Yes, *domine*. We left the sheets on the bed, in case you want to inspect them."

"That won't be necessary. Your word is good enough for me." He dissipated some of the tension with a smile. "We want to have a grandson soon. So, hopefully, it will be only nine months from now."

My heart skipped a beat. Was one supposed to get a woman pregnant on the first night? I had no idea how any of that worked. And I had no one to ask.

"Yes... let's hope so," I muttered.

"That's all I needed to know." He stood up and patted my shoulder. "Let's go join the ladies."

When we got to the kitchen, Caecilia and her mother were engaged in a lively conversation. I felt a twinge of jealousy at how well they got along.

"So here are the *domini,*" her mom said. "Just in time before their milk gets cold."

We sat on stools, me on Caecilia's side, and her father on her mother's side.

"Mother, before I forget," Caecilia said, taking a sip, "we'll need slaves to help us run the house."

"Of course, dear, we'll get you some. How many do you need? Would two men and two women suffice?"

"If you don't mind, we'd like to find them ourselves."

Puzzled, her mother looked at her husband, then back at her.

"Please don't look at me like that, Mother. Last night, Lucius and I discovered that we are very particular about our needs. We wouldn't be comfortable with people we didn't choose ourselves. Is that a problem?"

"No, darling, it's not a problem, but... Well, it's just a little unusual, don't you think, Marcus?"

"Very unusual. But if that's what they want, good luck!" He looked at us. "Do you know where to find them?"

"Not really... and that's one of the reasons we came to visit you so early... We'd like to start looking for them right away. Can you tell us where to go?"

"Of course," Marcus said. "I can come with you if you want."

"We would rather go ourselves," Caecilia said.

"These young couples…" Marcus said with a chuckle. "They think they can do it all on their own, but they will soon find out that there's nothing more valuable than good advice."

We all laughed.

"Let me at least get you some money." Marcus left the room and returned with a small velvet pouch and a sheet of papyrus. "This should be enough for four or five slaves. I wrote down the names and addresses of the traders I know. You'll have to haggle, though. You know how those foxes are. They'll try to rip you off if they see you have no experience."

"Don't worry, Father, we'll be careful," Caecilia said, getting up to give him a hug. "And now, I think we'd better get going, right, Lucius? We want to make sure we arrive early so that the best haven't been chosen yet."

We arrived at the first market on the list. Asking for the owner, we were directed to the *tablinum* of a corpulent man, who noisily consumed a bowl of *puls*.

"We're here," Caecilia said, assuming an air of importance, "looking for suitable slaves for our household."

The man hastily put away his bowl, wiping his mouth with his forearm, and gestured one of his workers to bring him a set of keys.

"We're here to serve you, fine people," he said in a rough voice. "May I ask your names?"

"My name is Lucius Cornelius, and this is my wife Caecilia," I said, extending my hand while suppressing my aversion to his foul odor. I had to maintain a pleasant demeanor, in case Renatus was there. "We just got married."

"Naturally," he said, reciprocating my handshake. "Congratulations! I know the joy of the early days of marriage. Lots of happiness, and lots of..." he added, making an obscene gesture with his hands. "It makes me happy to see young people starting their life together. Things change rapidly, so enjoy it while you can."

We followed him down a hallway and through a heavy iron door. A pungent smell struck me—a mixture of sweat, urine, and excrement. In a corner of my mind I harbored the hope that these places were not so grim and that the wretched were treated with at least a modicum of dignity, but my illusions were dashed as soon as we stepped through that door. The smell intensified the further we went in; I had to cover my nose with my tunic to avoid retching.

A varied assembly of men surrounded us—elderly, young, robust, and feeble—all shackled and bearing expressions of despair. But Renatus was not among them.

"I regret to inform you that we couldn't find anyone we liked," Caecilia said to the man after we had finished surveying the cells.

"That's unfortunate. Be sure to come back another day. We have new ones coming in constantly, you may find a more suitable one then."

"This is pointless. We're never going to find him," I said to Caecilia as we walked outside.

"We have just begun our search, Lucius. Don't fall into despair so soon."

We diligently visited all the markets listed by Marcus, and even ventured into others suggested by the slave traders themselves, only to meet with the same outcome. We even asked the traders directly if they had seen a slave matching Renatus's description in recent days, but among the hundreds of men, it was impossible for them to say for sure. We arrived home after dark, tired and frustrated.

Beneath a brilliant full moon in the midnight sky, I found myself climbing an eerily familiar rugged incline. A gust of wind forced me to grasp onto the rocks around me, my dirt covered feet struggling for support.

I crawled my way to the top, where a circular valley appeared, from which intense heat and a strong sulfurous smell emanated. At my back, boisterous waves crashed violently against a lighthouse shimmering in the distance. I retraced my steps, trying to descend to the forest on the mountain slopes, but the vastness of the landscape made me lightheaded.

"Lucius! Lucius!" Renatus's voice cried out.

"Renatus! Where are you?"

I changed directions and ran toward the center of the valley, where Renatus's voice had originated.

"Lucius! Help me! Please, help me!"

"Renatus, my love, where are you? I can't see you!"

The wind howled.

"Here!"

I looked behind me, and there he was, raising his chained hands toward me. Then the smoldering ground shook, and the earth opened up into a large crack. Renatus fell in, struggling to hold on to the edge with his bound hands.

"Lucius!"

I ran toward him, attempting to reach his hands, but hot molten rock spewed out, thwarting my efforts. My second attempt came too late; he had lost his grip and plunged into the incandescent pit.

I awoke with a scream, soaked in sweat and panting heavily.

"What happened?" Caecilia asked.

The words caught in my throat.

"It was just a nightmare, that's all,"

"It's Renatus, Caecilia. He's in danger, I know it!"

"Don't worry, we'll find him. We'll search the whole city if we have to, but I swear by Juno we'll find him," she said, hugging me.

I hugged her back. If I still believed in the gods, I'd thank them for putting such a good woman by my side.

21

A full week passed, during which we tried all the slave markets in Neapolis without success. We didn't know where else to search. Perhaps my father hadn't deceived me, and Renatus had already been shipped to the East. I felt tired and miserable; life had become an unbearable burden. And amid all this, Caecilia's parents insisted that we join them at a party.

The event was to take place at one of the opulent villas outside the walls of Neapolis, owned by one of the numerous aristocrats I now found contemptible. I didn't even know the *pater familias*, but we had to attend, as Caecilia's parents asserted that we were now a part of their social circle.

Caecilia wasn't particularly eager about attending either, but she mentioned that such social events were unavoidable, especially for a young couple like us. At our age, it was crucial to establish connections that could pave the way for our future endeavors.

Marcus had arranged for a coach to pick up the four of us around the *hora nona* and take us uphill to the Neapolitan countryside. The road was paved all the way to the villa, an unequivocal sign of wealth. It curved along the hillsides, offering a stunning view of the city walls to the north, of a row of lavish, coastal residences to the east, and of the port and its buzzing activity to the south. A cool breeze refreshed us through the open windows, as golden eagles wheeled above Mount Vesuvius.

We arrived at our destination after an hour or so, the sun shining brightly in the middle of the sky. The huge villa slumbered beneath the shade of giant umbrella pines and sprawled itself on a series of terraces facing the bay. Our carriage stopped by an arched gate set into a long high yellow wall. A smartly dressed porter welcomed us with a bow and instructed us to enter with our right foot first, so that we would have a lucky evening—something that almost made me roll my eyes.

In the center of the garden, under a rose-covered pergola, was a circular stone bench surrounding a marble fountain with a crouching sphinx as a base around which finches and magpies were singing. A cloister-covered walk ran along the walls. To the left was an entrance to a pomegranate orchard, which immediately brought back memories: this had been one of the villas where I had been taken to pick fruit. That time we had entered through a backdoor that led directly into the orchard, so although I had foreseen the luxury of the mansion, I didn't have the opportunity to experience it as I was doing now.

A tall white man with blue eyes and graying blond hair— clad in a sumptuous red Greek *synthesis*—and his wife, an elegantly attired middle-aged woman adorned with gold jewelry and precious stones, approached to welcome us.

"Dear Marcus," the man stated, shaking hands with our patriarch, "I'm delighted to have you and your family here. Did you have a pleasant journey?"

"Yes, dear Pompeius, everything went well. We're honored to be in your villa again, and well, my son-in-law for the first time."

Only that it wasn't my first time there.

The man turned to greet me, raising his eyebrows slightly. "Ah yes, Lucius, that is your name, correct?" he said, shaking my hand. "I'm so sorry that we couldn't attend your wedding ceremony. As your father-in-law must have told you, we were travelling in Sicilia at the time and—"

His words were abruptly cut off by the loud sound of a trumpet from behind.

"Stop, Pamphilus, stop! Don't blow that thing when I'm talking to my guests!" The musician apologized profusely and walked away. "Where were we?" he said, clasping his hands.

Pompeius and his wife, Fortunata, guided us through the garden, introducing us to their friends while narrating the architectural features and sculptures of their villa.

"Behold, my pride!" he exclaimed as we reached his fishpond, a sizable, yellow-painted concrete structure. "It draws water from the sea—my precious fishes couldn't live without it," he commented with a chuckle, "and it recycles it back through those canals," he added, pointing to the shore.

With evident delight, he continued to share the intricate workings of his fishpond, explaining every little detail as we walked around it.

"By the way, I must note that this is the sole pink bearded mullet farm in Neapolis. Look at these beauties, swimming about in happiness, oblivious to the fact that their destiny is to grace our plates any minute."

The guests burst into laughter.

He dipped his hand in and snatched one of the fish, which squirmed in his grip. "Aww you precious, struggling to live, but, no worries, I'm going to leave you alone another day," he said, returning it to the pond.

We admired the separate sections for shellfish, oysters, and eels as we strolled down a walkway with a mosaic floor in white and blue, embellished with sea creature designs.

"And now, take a gander at my baby here," he said, splashing the water. "Come on, sweetie, come greet my guests."

A head of dark blue and yellow emerged. It belonged to a moray eel adorned with a golden necklace and earrings. Pompeius offered it a small green fig.

"Look how beautiful you are," he remarked, gently tapping its head as it seized the fig with its fangs.

"And how tame," one of the guests observed.

"She knows she's loved. She wouldn't go back to the sea, even if she had the chance," Pompeius replied.

Beyond the ponds, a broad catwalk extended to a set of stairs, with one leading down to the seashore and the other ascending to the second level of his mansion, where a massive freshwater pool—approximately two hundred feet in length and fifty feet in width—was located. The pool lacked railings, and from a certain viewpoint, it appeared to seamlessly blend into the sea. I had no idea that such a construction was possible. Several men and women were inside, holding wine goblets.

"The water in this pool is sourced from the aqueduct and flows from the edge into a basin, where it is then pumped back up," Pompeius explained to a curious guest. "There's a drain that can be opened to clean it. There are only two such pools in the world, the other being in Persia."

"It's a wonderful construction," the man remarked, "very ingenuous indeed. I'm sure these pools will soon become very popular throughout the empire."

"The problem, as you can imagine, is that the maintenance cost is prohibitive. It's something only the emperors—or me—could afford," he said with a mischievous wink.

Marcus had shared some of Pompeius's story with me on the way from Neapolis. He was a freedman who had amassed his wealth through trade and astute investments. Marcus noted that while Pompeius certainly deserved every *sestertius* he had earned, he lacked the refined manners of high society, and at times he could come off as overly pedantic and arrogant. However, up until now, we had only witnessed his charming side.

After a while, we were ushered inside the villa, where we explored several rooms adorned with walls covered in breathtaking frescoes celebrating Greek architecture. These painting showcased colonnades, gates, shrines, and multi-story houses, complete with balconies and terraces—all rendered in vibrant gold, red, and green against a backdrop of blue skies.

Since it was still early, we were invited to partake in a bath to freshen up for dinner. We had anticipated this and had brough along fresh party clothes. The facilities were remarkably spacious, nearly comparable to the public baths in Pompeii, yet far cleaner and better maintained. Obviously, they showed much less wear and tear, given that they did not accommodate a daily crowd of bathers. We were separated by sexes, so I was accompanied by my father-in-law.

After the bath, the guests were offered grooming services, such as nail clippings, massages, and strigiling. Hard as it is to believe, some of the men didn't restrain their appetites and engaged in lewd behavior with the slaves providing these services, regardless of their gender.

I was appalled to witness such activities, especially given the early hour and the relatively low consumption of wine so far. I speculated that for these men, this might be the only opportunity to indulge their basest instincts before returning to the company of their wives. The presence of my father-in-law made me feel even more uncomfortable, and although he did not participate in such behavior, he didn't seem bothered by what was happening.

He and I proceeded to a smaller changing room, where we donned the *synthesis* robes we had brought. Before doing so, two slaves anointed us with mint-scented oil, although without the additional "comfort."

Later we reunited with our women outside of the ladies' *cubiculum*, a lavish room adorned with gold trim and brightly painted walls, where other women were busy with their make-up and styling their hair with braids, ribbons, hairpins, and curl extensions.

Caecilia was dazzling in her dark red stola, complemented by gold and ruby jewelry. Her parents and we were then ushered to the outdoor dining room, where appetizers were being served. On our way there, we encountered a slave, whose chest had been stripped naked, being led away to be whipped.

"*Domina*," he implored, kneeling before Caecilia, "I beg for your mercy! Please ask my master not to have me flogged!"

"Don't pay him any mind," the servant leading him interjected, "he broke two plates today; the master doesn't tolerate such inept behavior."

"I'll speak to Pompeius," Caecilia assured the unfortunate. "Leave this slave alone, I beg you," she asked the escort.

"But *domina*, you don't have to get into such trouble—"

"It's no trouble at all," I said. "We'll ask Pompeius to pardon him."

"Thank you, thank you!" the slave exclaimed, showering kisses on our feet. "The gods will show their mercy on you, lovely young couple."

"But we need to have a word with you first," Caecilia said to the man, signaling for him to get on his feet. "In private," she added, looking at his escort.

The escort bowed and left. Caecilia then asked her parents to proceed to the dining area and led the slave and me to a secluded corner outside. I looked around to make sure no one could see us.

"We've helped you, so now you must help us," she whispered.

"Whatever you need, divine Lady."

"We've been looking for a slave named Renatus. He's young, dark-skinned, and hails from Pompeii. We've tried all the slave markets in Neapolis with no luck. He was captured a month ago, and we were informed he was sold to the East, but we're not sure if this information is true. Have you by any chance heard of anyone by that name?"

The slave shrugged. "No, Mistress, I swear by Ra. His new owner may have renamed him, or he may not have named him at all."

"But do you know anything that could help us—anything at all?"

The man pondered for a minute. "Well, if you said that he was sold to the East... and that he was captured about a month ago... then, as long as he hasn't been taken overland, he must still be in Neapolis... You see, the only ship that sails East with slave cargo does so every two months or so..."

"Do you know who runs that trade?"

"Of course. Actually he's here at the party."

Our eyes brightened.

"Who is he?" I asked.

He led us to the courtyard.

"Do you see that man with the purple *synthesis* with golden embroidery? That's Pontius Heraclius, the owner of the ship. You can ask him when it will sail."

Now I was the one kissing the man's cheek.

"Oh, don't do that, young master. I'm not worthy."

"Yes, you are. You have no idea how grateful we are to you. Would you like to come work with us in our home?"

"It would be a great honor for me to serve such a worthy family. But I'm afraid that the master won't want to sell me…"

"We'll make sure he does." Caecilia kissed him on the cheek as well. "We'll take you with us as soon as possible. What's your name?"

"My name is Ramose, but you can call me whatever you want."

"Ramose it is," she said.

22

In a much better mood, we rejoined the party in an outdoor *triclinium* overlooking a lovely fountain. We were surrounded by about twenty other people, mostly older couples, some of which were acquainted to Caecilia. Appetizers—including bread, cheese, and fruit—had been served on a table floating on a central pool, while slaves brought us snow-cooled water and honeyed wine. However, shortly after settling down, it became evident that the experience would not be as pleasant as anticipated.

"So, is there a baby on the way?" one of the women asked Caecilia out of the blue.

How nonchalantly they think they can intrude into our private lives!

"We hope so," Caecilia replied, taking a sip of her goblet.

"Well, it's still not noticeable."

"Lydia, they only got married last month," her husband said.

"Oh, I know." She gave him a condescending look. "Don't worry, darling," she said, turning her cynical gaze back to Caecilia, "you'll soon be getting that nasty nausea and eating like a pig." She and other women chuckled. "Oh, and when you're nursing, your breasts will get so big and loose… and just like that your beauty will be gone. But it's all for the good of the family."

"Women breastfeeding are the most beautiful of all," I declared, not hiding my annoyance.

"You sure haven't been around a lot of breastfeeding women." She cackled.

Some of the guests joined in the laughter. This irritated me more than I could bear. Caecilia noticed and placed her reassuring hand on my forearm.

"I have the impression that I've seen you before," a man said to me.

"How could you?" his wife interjected. "We're not acquainted, dear. We weren't invited to their wedding."

"I know, darling, I'm not drunk nor stupid." He turned his gaze back to me. "But I could swear that I've seen you picking pomegranates in our orchard. Your red curls are hard to forget."

Gasps were followed by an awkward silence.

"I've never picked fruit in my life, *domine*," I lied.

"Of course, dear," his wife said, embarrassed.

"So, have you got a job already, Lucius?" said another man, biting into an apple.

"I'll start working with my father as soon as we finish arranging our new home." I wasn't entirely certain if I would, but that was the response they wanted to hear. I said it mostly to protect Caecilia, not wanting them to think her husband was a loafer.

"That will be very lucrative," the man said. "Assuming, of course, that you learn the ropes expeditiously. Law practice can be complicated, to say the least."

"Not for those with money," the previous man said.

"*Salve lucrum!*" one of the others proposed, raising his goblet.

"*Salve lucrum!*" the idiots repeated.

Fortunately for us, the conversation veered away from our personal matters and delved into politics, travel, hunting, and, above all, money. They boasted about the size of their villas, the duration of their vacations, the success of their businesses and the like. *Revolting*. How I understood Eusebius and Gaia now, and how I yearned to live a simple life like them.

After our evening was nearly ruined by the awful company at the round of appetizers, all the guests were called into the main ballroom—a large hall adorned with a series of frescoes depicting Pompeius as different heroes of Greek and Roman mythology, interacting with various gods and goddesses. In the center of the room stood a statue of Fortuna holding a cornucopia, with the three Fates at her feet, spinning a golden thread.

Several *triclinii* had been arranged to accommodate the guests, approximately two hundred people. We were guided to our divan, where, luckily, this time we were accompanied by nicer people. More food was served along with copious amounts of wine. The first course consisted of dormice battered in poppy-seeds and honey, hot sausages, dried plums, and pomegranate seeds—sourced from Pompeius's own courtyard, of course.

For entertainment, Pompeius had arranged a lineup of poets and singers accompanied by background musicians playing lutes, flutes, and harps. Additionally, two actors presented a short comedy. Pompeius personally visited each *triclinium* to ensure that all his guests were well attended to.

For the main course a peculiar feature was prepared, capturing everyone's attention. It involved several huge round tables, each with a platter divided into twelve sections, corresponding to each sign of the Zodiac. Each section contained food that was deemed appropriate for the specific sign. Slaves rolled each of these tables to every *triclinium*, and guests were asked their Zodiac sign and given a selection of food from the section corresponding to their sign. My section, Cancer, naturally contained crab legs, as well as lobster and other shellfish. However, Caecilia was disappointed to discover that Gemini's section contained only kidneys and testicles, so I offered her some of my crab.

During dinner, four dancers executed a choreographed performance to lively music, while more food was served alongside the remarkable Zodiac platter. The new offerings included suckling pig stuffed with minced lamb, coriander, and fennel; a mouthwatering hare stew with leek and carrot; and small animals fried in lard. Naturally, the ponds on Pompeius's estate provided an abundance of farmed fish, which was served in a flavorful garum sauce. To finish, a pie with a red almond paste crust and ricotta filling with candied fruit was served, accompanied by sweet wine.

We had a pleasant time chatting with our table neighbors. The wine was acting strongly on me, and I ended up being more affectionate with Caecilia than is socially permissible, but no one seemed to mind. Although my mood had lightened, it worried me a little that we still hadn't had a chance to talk to the ship owner who could take us to Renatus. As the evening drew to a close and some guests excused themselves to retire to their designated *cubicula*, I told Caecilia that we needed to pull ourselves together and locate the man. We found him extremely inebriated, engrossed in animated banter with other men.

"Pardon me, *domine*. Would it be possible to have a word with you? It's an important matter."

He excused himself from his companions and joined us.

"Pontius Heraclius, it's a pleasure to meet you," I said, offering a handshake.

"…and your name is?" he inquired, shaking my hand, and arching his eyebrow.

"I'm Lucius Cornelius, and this is my wife Caecilia. We've been wanting to talk to you all night."

"Nice to make your acquaintance, young folks," he said, slinging his arm around my shoulder. The wine had certainly taken a positive toll on him. "You only had to come over if you wanted to chat. I'm not an arrogant prick like some other wealthy fellows around here." He laughed. "What brings you to me?"

"You see, Heraclius," Caecilia said, "we are a new household in need of slaves, and we've heard that you own a large ship that transports many of them to the East."

EVAN D. BERG

His expression shifted to one of suspicion. "Why don't you go to the slave markets?"

"We've already been there but haven't found any we like," Caecilia said. "So, we thought we'd check to see if we have better luck with those being shipped overseas. It seems that all the good slaves are sent to the East."

"You're mistaken. The finest slaves remain here. Only the useless, those nobody wants, are sent abroad."

If only I could tell him that a very able man might be among those slaves, just because an evil monster had arranged it.

"We'd still like to give it a try," I said. "Could you tell us when the next ship will sail so we can take a look?"

"Folks, you don't understand. Those slaves have already been sold and paid for. They're not available."

"We're willing to offer substantial compensation if we find the right slaves," Caecilia said. "We simply can't have the wrong people working in our *domus*."

"And you think you will find the 'right slaves' among the wretched?" He laughed and took another gulp of his wine. "Alright. The ship will sail next Friday at dawn. But I must warn you that I won't be there to help you. I own the ship, but I don't personally oversee its operations. You're free to go there and look around as much as you like. I'll give my men your names, so they know that you've had a conversation with me."

Caecilia and I exchanged ecstatic glances.

"Thank you, Heraclius, thank you very much." I shook his hand vigorously.

We left the man in bewilderment, wondering why we were so excited about checking out leftover slaves. However, on our way to our guestroom, the sight of another figure paralyzed me.

"What's wrong?" Caecilia said.

I couldn't believe my eyes. I pointed at a bulky, well-dressed man cheerfully conversing with two ladies. "That's Albus," I uttered in a trembling voice, "the man who kidnapped me."

Caecilia gaped, her eyes wide. "What are you talking about?"

I rushed toward the man.

"Lucius, what are you doing!?"

A flash of dread appeared in his eyes as I stood before him. "And who are you, young man?" he said in a conceited patrician tone. "May I ask why you come to us so suddenly, like a villain in the street?"

"You know all about villains in the street, don't you? Because you're one of them."

"Excuse me? I don't know who you think you are, but I must ask you to leave us alone. My wife and her mother need not suffer such impertinence."

"They will suffer more than that when they find out who you really are," I spouted before walking away.

I returned to Caecilia, trembling.

"You have a lot to explain to me."

"Let's go to our room. I'll tell you everything."

23

The subsequent days in Neapolis crept by at an excruciating pace. On Thursday night, I wanted to head to the port and wait for the sunrise, but Caecilia persuaded me to be reasonable. Lying in bed next to her that night, sleep eluded me anyway. The eager anticipation of reuniting with Renatus, holding him in my arms, and expressing how much I had missed him kept me restless. Simultaneously, the fear of not finding him haunted the depths of my mind, and I grappled with the challenge of pushing those thoughts aside.

It took us about half an hour to reach the port. Armed with daggers and a purse of gold, we arrived just before dawn and saw a multitude of ships ready to sail, mostly merchant vessels. As we walked around, we came across one where men bound in chains formed a line. My heart raced as I strode past them, scrutinizing their faces one by one, Caecilia following close behind.

Suddenly, there he was—Renatus, appearing before my eyes like a beacon in the twilight. He was standing in line like the others, his hands held in chains, wearing a ragged brown tunic. He looked thinner, but the muscles of his arms remained as strong as ever; no wonder they had deemed him fit for heavy labor. Although his face bore the signs of the trials of captivity, it still exuded the familiar warmth that had charmed me since our first encounter.

"Renatus!" I exclaimed as I rushed toward him.

He instantly recognized my voice and smiled at me in a way I'll never forget. I wrapped him in a loving embrace, bathed in the muted hues of dawn, amid the confused gaze of the captives.

"I knew you'd find me."

I was naively jolting his shackles when one of the handlers came up to from behind.

"Hey! You! What do you think you're doing?"

"There's been a mistake, this boy is my cousin! We're from Pompeii. The man who sold him had no rights over him."

"Don't feed me that nonsense. These men are slaves and are slated to work in the Greek mines," he replied, as Caecilia arrived.

"Are you in charge here?" I asked. "We've already spoken to the ship's owner, Pontius Heraclius. He assured us he would give his men notice of our arrival."

"How do you know his name? You couldn't possibly know him personally. Now get out of here before I lose my patience, and—"

"Perhaps you've heard of my father, Marcus Caecilius Iucundus," Caecilia interjected. The man fell silent. "Allow me to introduce myself," Caecilia said with her most ladylike manners. "I am this young man's wife. And my father will be greatly displeased if he learns that his son-in-law's request has been ignored."

"What proof do you have that you are Marcus Caecilius's daughter?"

"This." She displayed her family ring.

He hesitated for a moment. "Come with me."

"He must come with us too," I said.

"He stays here."

Caecilia and I followed him, my gaze fixed on Renatus for as long as possible during the walk. A few moments later, we reached a makeshift shack on the shore.

"Captain, these folks want to talk to you."

The captain, seated with a goblet of wine in hand, scowled at us.

"What do you want? Hurry it up, I don't have time to waste," he said, taking a swig.

"We're interested in purchasing one of your slaves," Caecilia said.

The man raised his eyebrows. Caecilia showed him the purse.

"Which one?"

"His name is Renatus," I said.

"The slaves have no names. Point him out." He led us outside.

"Him," I indicated, as he came to our sight. "The young one with strong arms and the brown tunic."

"That one is expensive. I doubt you have what he's worth."

Caecilia tossed the bag at him. "That should do. We can buy five healthy slaves with that money."

"This is not the market, lady," he said with a grimace. He opened the bag with a deadpan expression. "Why do you want him precisely?"

"That's none of your business," Caecilia said. "Now, order your men to release him."

"Not so fast. What if I don't want to sell him?"

"Then I'll see to it that my father speaks to Pontius Heraclius to have you removed."

The man started laughing but fell silent when she displayed her family ring.

"Alright. Paulus, get the key and give these people the slave they want."

"Faster!" I urged the man, who walked as one in no hurry. The captain went back to his shack.

Unable to contain my excitement, I showered Renatus with kisses the moment he was freed, to the scornful gaze of the henchman.

"Let me introduce you to Caecilia."

"*Salve*," he greeted her, then he looked back at me. "Is she... your wife?"

"Yes..." I replied.

"And no..." Caecilia chimed in with a wink.

"We'll explain everything when we get home," I said. "Let's go!"

"I haven't had a meal like this in weeks, thank you Caecilia." Renatus licked the spoon after devouring his hearty soup.

We indulged in a lengthy post-dinner conversation, reclining closely to each other—with me in the middle—on one of the divans of the *triclinium*, surrounded by amphorae of wine. Caecilia—warm and cheerful—contributed to the atmosphere, reminiscent of childhood friends.

"You're so lucky that your father chose this lovely lady to be your wife," Renatus said, pouring more wine for us.

"Yes, I am," I said, hugging her. "He has no idea of how things turned out."

"My parents were in on it too," Caecilia said, affectionately leaning on my shoulder. "This was their grand plan for a political alliance. Before the wedding I was outraged that they were trying to use me to advance their social power, but now I'm glad it happened."

"But I'm sure your family are good people," Renatus said to Caecilia. "I wish they could meet my parents; I'm sure they would get along very well."

"Unfortunately, I can't say the same," I said. "And it makes me really sad."

"But hey, look on the bright side," Renatus said. "If your parents were good people, we would have never met."

"That's true." I gave him a peck. "Cheers to that!"

We clinked our copper goblets and sipped.

"I think it's safest for you to stay here with us," Caecilia said. "I don't think Lucius's father suspects that you're still in Neapolis, but it's better not to risk it. Besides… I'm sure you want to be together."

"Oh Caecilia," I said, teary-eyed. "You're such a blessed creature. How can we pay you for what you're doing for us?"

"You don't have to pay me. I'm happy to be your friend."

Renatus reached out to hold her hand. "Thank you, dearest of friends."

I embraced them for a long time.

"But there are many things we have to think about," I said, releasing them. "I'm sure your parents would like to see the slaves we bought," I said to Caecilia. "Now we don't even have the money. Also, where can Renatus stay? They will check every room…"

"We'll come up with a solution."

"Besides… Everyone expects us to produce an heir soon."

"I know, and I hope you realize that 'everyone' is not only our parents but society in general. You heard that woman at the party."

"Let's not bring up someone so unpleasant. And you're right. I hadn't told you this, but your father expressed his hope that I did my job well, and that you're already pregnant. Do women really conceive on the first try? Do you know anything about that, Renatus?"

"I'm not sure… but I can ask Mom."

"Good. And that reminds me that we still have to inform your parents that we found you."

A few hours later, Caecilia retired to sleep in the main *cubiculum*, allowing me to join Renatus in the slave quarters. Fully naked, we cuddled, with him behind me. I hadn't felt so safe and warm since our time at his parents' villa. So much had transpired since then: the mishap with Eusebius, my sexual escapades in Pompeii, my abduction, delving into the philosophy, the apparition of my father… and now the circle seemed to have closed, albeit not quite.

He kissed my neck and caressed my chest.

"I don't know about this, Renatus."

"You don't want it?"

"I want it. I want it so much. But I feel bad doing this under Caecilia's roof. I don't think it's right."

"You think she doesn't know we're going to do this?"

"Well, maybe, but still… I don't want to disrespect her."

"I think we would disrespect her more if we're not comfortable under her protection."

Passion grew in his manhood between my asscheeks. I trapped it and massaged it.

"Ohh, man…" he whispered.

I turned around to kiss him. He reciprocated my passion, instantly erasing all the time we had been apart.

"Alright, you win. As long as we don't make too much noise…"

He slid his lips down my neck and chest and bit my nipples lightly.

"Wait…"

He stopped, startled.

"Don't you want to practice some of that tantric sex?"

"I've got no patience for that," he said, rubbing his cheeks against my belly.

Quivering, I stopped him and pulled him near my face. We kissed again and touched each other desperately, wanting to melt into each other.

He made me lie on my back as he knelt in front of me. He pushed my legs back as he leaned over my torso, resting his steel-hard cock on mine as he kissed me. A trickle of his precum fell onto my stomach. Then he straightened his back and pinched my hole with the mushroom-shaped head of his cock.

He entered me slowly, carefully, as during our first time. Leaning toward me, he kissed my neck, brushing my jaw with his beard. His movements were steady, but not fast, giving me time to get used to his vigor again. My asshole was his and his cock was mine; it couldn't be otherwise.

He kept thrusting, a little faster now, and then stopped. Going back to a kneeling position—he left his hard cock inside—and spread my legs wider. With his cock almost all the way out with each thrust, I could enjoy his full length with each penetration. *What a lucky young man I am to be loved like this.*

Then he made me lie on my side and he positioned himself behind me. He lifted one of my legs to make room for his manhood and continued to hammer my hole this way. I touched my balls and started to jerk myself off, but he pulled my hand away from my cock and did the job himself. He was now pleasuring my ass and my cock at the same time. I wanted to die of pleasure.

"Oh Renatus, I can't hold it, I'm going to cum!"

He kept stroking me harder until I shot my sperm onto the bed and floor as I moaned in ecstasy. Even more excited, he continued to increase the pace of his movements. Soon I felt his jism inside me as he let out his manly moans without letting go of my dripping cock. When he was done, he leaned over, resting his weight on me, his cum-soaked hand still touching my now shriveling cock. Our breathing, at first heaving and then gradually returning to a normal rhythm, was completely synchronized. In the midst of this indescribable bliss, it wasn't long before we fell asleep.

I woke up in a different place, still cradled in Renatus's arms, lying naked on scorching hot soil.

"Renatus, wake up." I nudged him gently.

He opened his eyes. "Where are we?"

A powerful rumble spurred us to hastily rise as a tremor shook the ground. We tried to run but the earth was determined to engulf us. Leading the way, I seized Renatus by the forearm, pulling him downhill. However, a rock, ejected from the depths of the mountain, propelled him away from me and into a hole.

"Lucius! Run, save yourself!"

"No, I'm coming for you!"

"No! Leave me! Get out of here fast, you fool!"

I kept running toward him, but he disappeared before my eyes.

"Renatus, no!" I woke up with a scream.

"Lucius, what happened?" He slipped his arm around my shoulders.

I gazed into his confused eyes. "I... keep having nightmares about Mount Vesuvius." I struggled to steady my breathing. "I thought it was because you were in danger, but now..." I surrendered myself in his arms. "I'm afraid of that mountain, Renatus. I'm so afraid of it. I think it's alive and it hates us all!"

Book Five

24

A few weeks of relative tranquility went by. With funds provided by my father, we acquired some slaves, both male and female. Ramose was, of course, the first addition to our household; we sent for him right after rescuing Renatus. We did our best to treat all our slaves as family, and, truth be told, I found their presence more comforting than that of our actual families, especially my own.

Yet, my father's influence lingered as a constant threat. *If only he could have been content now that I was married.*

"So you work with your hands now? That's new," he said as he entered our home while I was helping the slaves build a table.

Luckily, Renatus was not with us. After a few unannounced visits in which he had almost caught us, we had resolved that during the more precarious hours of the day he would stay in the inner rooms.

"What do you need, Father? As you can see, I'm busy and—"

"To talk to you. In the *tablinum*."

I despised how he moved around my *domus* as if it was his own. Granted, he had paid for it, but that didn't give him the right to encroach on the privacy we deserved as a married couple.

We walked through the garden, where Caecilia was tending to her tasks. He exchanged greetings with her along the way. Once in the *tablinum*, he sat on my side of the table. Even in my own house he was the boss.

"You look happy. It seems you've been enjoying yourself, am I right? Didn't I tell you that married life is the best?"

"Why are you here? Get straight to the point and spare me the small talk." The sound of my own voice surprised me.

He looked at me with a hint of indignation. "You've been living off the dowry for a while, but that won't last forever. You'll have to start working soon if you want to support your wife… and the baby I expect is on the way."

A flush of heat spread across my face. Fortunately, we had already received Gaia's letter, in which she detailed that it's common for women not to conceive on the first night. Many, she mentioned, sought remedies like herbs and prayers—the latter, she clarified, being superstition—to achieve that purpose. She assured us not to worry, emphasizing that despite my father's pressure, any married individual would understand the variability of such matters.

"We don't know yet, Father," I uttered nervously. "I can assure you that we've been trying—"

"But are you sure you're trying it through the right hole?" he said with a smirk.

My father's insolence never failed to astonish me. "What are you talking about?"

"Well, given your... tendencies... I was thinking you might find satisfaction more readily through the back door... It's not a bad idea to take her from behind once in a while if that excites you... just make sure to hit the right hole as often as possible."

I couldn't bear to listen to any more of this vile conversation. I was on the verge of shouting at him to leave. "Understood. Anything else?"

"Yes. On the subject of your career, I expect you to begin attending my practice from tomorrow onward. Becoming a lawyer is not easy. You're not an idiot, but it will take you years to establish independence and cultivate your own client base. I'll provide you with a modest salary with which you can feed your family."

Modest. "And what if I don't want to be a lawyer?"

He chuckled. "Then what do you want to be? A carpenter?"

"I've already told you. I want to be an artist."

He burst into laughter—that obnoxious, boisterous laughter that ruffled my feathers. He wiped away the tears streaming down his face from the intensity of his amusement.

"That's enough, Father, if you've only come to my *domus* to mock me, you can leave now."

He fixed his gaze on me once more, his lizard eyes ablaze with terrifying intensity. "Don't make a fool of yourself. Artists are the dregs of society. Only losers and pretenders go that way. A son of mine will seek respect for himself."

"How can you denigrate artists, when your home is adorned with breathtaking frescoes and quaint niches?"

"Affluent people may like art, but we loathe artists and their extravagant lifestyle. Besides, don't think they make that much money. And all that matters in this life is money, my Son—money and prestige."

"I don't agree with that."

"You'll agree soon enough. And don't make things difficult for yourself. If you choose not to join my practice, there's another option."

I stared at him in dread.

"The military. I can arrange your recruitment in no time."

"You can't do that. You didn't join the military yourself."

"Because I chose to be a lawyer. It's one of the two for our class, Son. You decide." He rose to leave. "And I suppose by now you've forgotten all about your…" he said, his face contorting into a grimace of disgust, "former love interest?"

I felt an urge to leap at him and throttle him. I was so enraged that my mind went blank, unable to conjure a response.

A sinister smile crept across his face. "You'll get over it. And don't forget… if your deviant urges get the better of you … the second hole…"

He departed, closing the door behind him. Caecilia joined me a few minutes later, and I sought solace in her comforting embrace.

I had no choice but to start attending my father's practice. We began the day early reviewing documents, and then he made me gobble up all that stupid legal jargon I detest. "If you continue to show proficiency," he had said, "I'll entrust you with some minor cases soon." As if I cared.

One of the few things that I liked about returning to my old home was the opportunity to visit my mother, although I saw her with different eyes now. She had been the only free woman I was close to during my childhood, and she embodied the qualities I grew up associating with womanhood: docility, submissiveness, compliance. But now that I had met two other markedly different women, Gaia and Caecilia, I had come to realize the diminutive role she played in our household.

I was unsure whether my mother had been compelled to marry my father—as is often customary in families of our social standing—or if she had ever truly loved him. Those facets of their marriage remained obscured to me as I was growing up. My father represented the authority both my mother and I obeyed, and neither of us received much love or tenderness from him. Reflecting on it, I couldn't bring myself to believe that my mother had ever loved him. He was not a bad looking man; it was his personality that made him abominable.

This morning, as I sifted through the papyri my father had left me with, my mother entered the *tablinum*.

"So proud of my boy now being a part of the family practice," she said, placing her hands on my shoulders.

"It's not easy, Mother. And it's also terribly boring."

"But it's a sure way to establish yourself in society. Soon, clients will seek you out like your father... and you'll be famous for winning difficult cases, just like him."

That's because he's so ruthless. I know I don't have that in me.

She moved to the front side of the desk. "Can we have a little conversation, Lucius?"

"Sure, Mother," I replied, relieved at the opportunity to escape the tedious documents. "Would you like to go to the garden?"

She nodded, took my arm, and we strolled quietly under the clay portico and behind the columns that formed the peristyle. The walls reminded me of how hypocritical my father had been when he belittled artists and yet surrounded himself by their precious work. We settled on one of the benches as birds sang and drank water from the fountain.

"Your Father mentioned that you still hold the idea of wanting to be an artist."

"Did he tell you about our conversation at my home?"

"Of course. He never keeps anything from me. That's what has constituted the strength of our marriage."

"Do you really trust him, Mother?"

She gazed at me with pleading eyes. "Why shouldn't I? He has never deceived me."

I believed her. My father could be a real asshole, but he wasn't a liar.

"He has even confided in me with his deepest secrets."

Those words caught me off guard. My blood ran cold at the prospect of what those secrets might entail. Had he been involved in something sinister? I couldn't resist the opportunity to find out. "What secrets, Mother?"

She took my hands and sighed. "How's your married life going? Are you happy?"

"Yes, Caecilia is a truly wonderful woman," I said, irritated by the abrupt change of topic.

"Have you come to love her already?"

I was silent for a minute, trying to discern the intent behind her words. "Yes, of course." *As a sister.*

"I'm glad to hear that. A good marriage is possible even… under special circumstances…"

"Why do you speak in riddles, Mother? You're making me worried."

"There's nothing to worry about, Son, nothing at all, it's just… never mind. I'm getting old, and sometimes I say silly things…"

"What you're saying isn't silly, just a little strange. Can you get to the point, please?"

She sighed deeply. "That boy your father took away from you… You loved him, didn't you?"

I felt a chill. What did she know?

"Sure, Mother… in the short time I got to know him, I developed a sincere affection for him."

"What kind of affection…? That of a brother?"

"No, not the affection of a brother," I replied, my voice trembling. There no point in lying; they had surely already talked about it.

She nodded with a faint smile. "We knew it. That's why your father separated you from him. He knows that this kind of situation never comes to a good end."

"And how exactly does he know that?" I mustered the courage to ask.

My mother gazed at me with peculiar eyes, holding my hands for an eternity. "Because he's of the same ways as you."

The serenity with which she uttered those words was frightening. I must have shown great anxiety, because she rushed to try to calm me down, gently cupping my face in her hands.

"Don't worry, Son... it's still possible to lead a happy life with a caring, submissive woman by your side... someone who wouldn't challenge you even if she discovers the truth. That's one of the reasons why your father chose Caecilia for you."

"She's not... submissive," I said, not hiding my revulsion at the word. "She cares about me, she really does. And I've told her everything already."

"Just like your father told me," she said, glancing away, unable to hide a certain bitterness in her voice. She smiled and looked back at me. "What I really wanted to tell you is that it's still possible for you to get her pregnant. Your father did it with me. Think about that boy all you want when you're lying with her... but be sure to fulfill your duty. Even if you have only one child, it would be enough to save face."

To save face. I stood up, enraged. "I can't do that, Mother. I can't make love to a woman while I'm thinking of a man. It's disgusting and dishonest."

"Do it for her sake," she said, rising. "A woman deserves her husband's passion. Consider it a favor."

"I don't think she cares much for it. And I sincerely doubt she would want it as a favor."

"Perhaps she says that to spare your feelings."

"How do you know what's in her mind?"

"I'm a woman as well. We, women, have our own needs. It's not just men who enjoy themselves in bed."

"I have a favor to ask, Mother. Please refrain from meddling in my married life. We'll navigate our own solutions."

"We want grandchildren," she shrieked. "It's your duty to provide them for us. And more than one if the first is a female."

So, that's what it all boils down to—the continuation of the family line. "I'm in no obligation to provide anything. Now, if you'll excuse me, I have to get back to work."

I strode back to the *tablinum*. All of a sudden, legal documents became a genuine source of solace for me.

In the evening, Renatus discovered me pacing anxiously across our *cubiculum*.

"*Salve*, love," he said, putting his arm around my shoulders. "What's wrong?"

I let myself be carried away by his comforting embrace for a few minutes, and then led him to sit on the bed. I recounted the conversation with my mother and the repugnant expectations my parents held, despite being aware of my true nature. I also unveiled the secret my mother had disclosed about my father.

"Well, it's not surprising at all, many men who strongly oppose same-sex love often have something to hide."

"So, what is to be done, is there any remedy for this in the philosophy?"

Renatus pondered the question for a moment.

"Three things come to my mind: The first, you've already done—sharing your problems with a friend. Remember that even though we love each other, we're still the best friends in the world."

I smiled.

"Second: I believe you recognize that these are their expectations, not yours. Currently, we find ourselves in a compromised situation because we still don't have financial stability, but with hard work, this circumstance will soon improve. For now, it's crucial to concentrate on your inner tranquility and avoid being overwhelmed by negative emotions. Focus solely on what you can control and refrain from attempting to alter the attitudes of your parents."

He paused a little.

"Third: Art and recreation can help. I think you and Caecilia should attend comedy shows or poetry recitations; it can help you forget our troubles and temporarily soothe your soul."

"But what about you, wouldn't you like to attend?"

"It's too risky. No one should see us together."

My expression saddened.

"Don't worry about me. I'm happy if you're happy," he said, gently touching my face in an attempt to bring a smile. "Besides, I'm thinking of a fourth way, in which I could participate…"

"And what is it?"

"A lot of lovemaking… and a little wine."

25

When I shared Renatus's proposal with Caecilia, she suggested an even better idea. We would all attend the theater, not in Neapolis, but in Pompeii. We could go there every weekend; we didn't need anyone's permission. To avoid compromising Eusebius and Gaia, Caecilia and I planned to stay at one of the many guest houses, while Renatus could take advantage of the occasion to stay with his parents and sleep in his own *cubiculum*.

We arranged for a carriage to pick up the three of us at our *domus*. The driver had no knowledge of Renatus, and there was no way for him to suspect that he was anything more than just a slave in our service.

When we arrived at Eusebius's *domus*, Gaia opened the door. Without delay, she enveloped Renatus in a motherly hug, tears of joy running down her face. Eusebius followed, warmly embracing his son, his eyes also brimming with tears.

"Thank you for rescuing our son."

"My life also depended on it," I said.

It was heartwarming to see Gaia and Caecilia holding hands—evidently Gaia already cherished her as a daughter.

"Come in please," Gaia said. "You must be very tired. How did you make it here?"

We told them about Renatus's idea for us to have some fun, and how Caecilia gave it a whirl.

"You've become a team now," Gaia said. "I'm thrilled for all of you. Our family is finally expanding."

"By the way," I said, "there's one more person I'd like you all to meet. He's a friend I made at the retreat: his name is Basileus, lives here in Pompeii, and would be a great addition to our 'team' as Gaia called it." I smiled at her. "He asked me to visit him whenever I was in Pompeii, but with everything that's happened I haven't even had the time to send him a letter. I have the directions to his home. Why don't you all rest here while I go and look for him?"

With everyone's agreement, I set off for the streets. I had to ask for help a couple of times to locate Basileus's home, but eventually, I found it. From the outside, it appeared like a typical house with white walls and red dados, but the moment the slave opened the door and guided me into the atrium, I could tell that these people could be counted among the wealthiest in Pompeii.

"*Salve*, dear friend," Basileus said, approaching me with a warm hug. "You're here at last. I thought you'd never come to visit me."

"You have no idea about everything that has happened," I replied, reciprocating his hug. "I could tell you about it for hours."

"You can give me a summary."

"Do you have time to come with me now? I want to introduce you to Renatus and to my wife."

"Your wife?"

"Yes. It's not as bad as it sounds. I'll tell you all about it on the way."

"But let's grab a honeyed ice first."

We walked cheerfully down the streets as we talked, mostly me sharing the news.

"Wow, all that sounds really crazy," he said when we got to the ice shop. "But I'm glad it all worked out well for you."

"There's one thing that still bothers me that I haven't told you about."

Two honeyed ices," he said to the vendor. "They're on me, *amice.*

The vendor handed us the delicious snacks, and we resumed our walk in the sunshine.

"During that dinner at the villa, I caught sight of a man who still gives me nightmares."

"Your dad?" he joked.

"Worse... Albus, the man who kidnapped me."

Basileus almost dropped his ice. "And what did you do?"

"Not much. I just threatened him in front of his wife and mother-in-law that I was going to expose him. But I don't really know how to do it."

"He surely must have government connections. He couldn't run a sex slavery trade without them."

"But there must still be law-abiding citizens who would want to have him prosecuted."

He considered for a minute. "Yes, that might be true. He's been operating in the shadows, but if his schemes come to light, he might not be able to escape the law."

"I wonder how we can uncover him."

"I don't know," he said, taking a lick of his honeyed ice. "But my parents know a lot of people in the city administration. Maybe they can help…"

"Don't tell your parents, please. I'm embarrassed enough sharing it with you."

"But how can we get help if you don't want to tell anyone?"

"We need to find someone who doesn't know either of us, but who has a great zeal for justice."

"And we also need to gather evidence to incriminate him."

"Do you have any ideas on how to do that?"

"I'm thinking of something… Give me a week or two, and I'll come up with a plan."

"Thank you Basileus. I knew I could count on you, dear friend."

A couple of hours later, I returned to Eusebius's *domus* with the handsome young man. It was evident that he made an immediate impression on Caecilia, who looked at him in a way she never looked at me. It hadn't crossed my mind that Caecilia was the one without a partner in our team. But that problem could be solved now. Basileus's countenance didn't change much, but perhaps it was out of respect, given that she was legally my wife.

The rest of the day was amazing. The six of us strolled the streets together, stopped at a *thermopolium* for a bite, and watched street performances by dancers, mimes, and musicians. We enjoy each other's company, like a real family.

In the evening, we left Basileus at his home and walked with Eusebius, Gaia, and Renatus back to their residence, exchanging a brief farewell, as Caecilia and I needed to check in at our guest house.

I was brimming with happiness when we returned to Neapolis on Sunday. However, Monday morning came, and I had to go back to my father's *tablinum*.

He entered as he always did, without knocking, and placed his hands on the desk.

"I know you went to Pompeii over the weekend."

"Is there a problem with that?" I asked, meeting his gaze.

He smirked. "Why go there when we have plenty of entertainment here in Neapolis?"

"Now you want to dictate my leisure hours too?"

"I just found it a little odd, that's all." His fingers fidgeted on the desk. "You don't have any funny business going down there, do you?"

"Like what?" I asked, though I knew where he was going.

"Like a catamite lover."

His blunt statement infuriated me. "No, why would I? I'm a married man now—isn't that what you wanted? Besides, my wife is always with me. When do you think I would have the opportunity to engage in something like that behind her back?"

"I'm well aware of what happens in those baths over there. You could very well go back to your crimes while she's on the women's side."

"You have a very active imagination, don't you, Father?" I said, walking toward him. "If this reassures you: no, we haven't been to the baths in Pompeii."

"You'd better not. I have eyes everywhere. Don't think for a moment that I wouldn't find out if you lie."

He was about to leave the room, when I asked, "Why are you doing this to me, Father? Is it because you're just like me?"

He turned around, his expression a mix of rage and disgust. "How dare you insinuate something like that, you bastard."

"I'm not insinuating. And since you called me a bastard, let me ask you this... Are you really my father? Or was my mother already pregnant when you married her?"

He approached me and slapped my face hard. "Don't you dare to be so insolent, or you'll be without a job and the means to find another."

"If you want to fire me, go ahead. It would be a favor, as I don't want to be here," I said, shoving the papyri off the desk. "I hate you, you have no idea how much I hate you!"

He headed for the door again, but I couldn't let him leave without letting it all out. "You're jealous, aren't you? Jealous that I've done with a man what you wish you would have done. Jealous because a man truly loved me." I paused, gazing firmly at his astonished face. "Live with that, Father. Live with the fact that I had the love you only dreamed of having."

I rejoiced in watching him swallow hard. "I'll keep going to Pompeii whenever I want," I said, leaving the *tablinum*, and slamming the door.

26

My father didn't mention our visits to Pompeii again, so two Fridays later, we hit the road once more. Although I was always on the look for anyone tailing us, I wasn't going to let apprehension ruin the fun.

Caecilia, Renatus and I arrived in the afternoon at Eusebius's *domus*, where a cheerful Gaia greeted us. "Dear ones, guess what? We have a special treat for you today. A Greek theater company is in town, and they'll be performing their latest comedy today. Would you like to join us?"

"Of course," I said. "It sounds like a lot of fun. Let's bring Basileus too."

"And you know what's the best? They're Epicureans," Gaia said, winking, "so we're in for some delightful fun at the gods' expense."

"Isn't that a bit risky?" Caecilia asked. "I mean, wouldn't people be offended?"

"Not in this town, darling," Gaia replied. "Not everyone here is an Epicurean, but we're well tolerated. Those who disapprove simply won't attend."

I hurried to Basileus's residence, aware that time was limited before the performance began. Gasping for breath, I knocked on the door, and Basileus emerged with a suspicious expression, glancing both ways down the street.

"Hurry, come in! I have something to tell you."

I entered, a bit concerned that any delay might cause us to be late for the theater.

"I've been visiting the Sarno baths."

I frowned. "Why in the world would you go there? That's where—"

"Precisely. And I've been keeping an eye on Albus. I know when he usually goes there and his typical activities inside."

"Why didn't you tell me what you were planning to do? I would have—"

"Advised against it, I know. But this is the only way. We have to catch him in the act of kidnapping a boy so we can turn him over to the *vigiles*."

"And how exactly are we going to do that?"

"There's something else you need to know. And please, no lectures," he said, looking at me sternly. "I've been teasing him."

"Basileus, don't you realize how dangerous that is? He could have already kidnapped you, and we might never hear from you again."

"I understand the danger, and don't worry, I've been cautious. I've simply made him aware of my presence and dropped subtle hints that I'm interested in him. I think he's noticed me. He hasn't approached me yet, but I know that will happen eventually."

"So what's the plan?"

"He should be there right now. He was, last Saturday. Let's go, together we have a good chance of catching him."

"But Basileus, this requires more planning than just showing up. Besides, I had come to invite you to a theatrical performance that—"

"Do you really want to catch him or not? It's a prime opportunity, Lucius. We can watch the play another day."

"But they'll be worried if we don't show up…"

"We'll explain it to them later."

"Yeah, and they'll be upset that we didn't include them in our plan."

"Alright, leave, if that's what you want. But perhaps later I won't be inclined to assist you."

I considered for a minute. "Alright, *amice*. I understand the effort you've been making to catch this criminal. I just wish you had told me about it."

A few minutes later, we arrived at the Sarnos.

"I'm still not convinced that what we're doing is right," I said. "We can still reconsider and go to the theater."

"Don't be silly, we're almost there," Basileus said.

We arrived at the entrance, and immediately, unpleasant memories flooded my mind—not only of my kidnapping but also of my out-of-control behavior with Hector. The mere thought that one of the men who had fed my guts with their seed had been Albus filled me with disgust.

"Alright, here's the plan. We know his modus operandi. This time I'm going to hint harder that I want to play with him. Circle around the block to the back door that leads to the alley, which we know is the route he uses to take his victims. Locate a couple of *vigiles* to apprehend him and wait for us there. We'll be out in no less than an hour."

"I still believe this is extremely risky, Basileus. What if he wants to have sex with you there instead of taking you to his lair?"

"He rarely has sex there, and when he has it's mostly in groups, like what he had with you."

"And you had to remind me."

"Sorry, *amice*. Anyway, are you in?"

"I guess I don't have a choice."

Locating *vigiles* willing to act on the account of a criminal pervert operating in the baths wasn't easy. Evidently, many of the armed men in the area had already been bribed or were possibly involved in the business. I had to walk a bit farther in the direction of the forum to find *vigiles* who demonstrated greater concern for the law, particularly when it came to sex crimes.

I returned to the baths with two officers, but two hours passed with no sign of Basileus.

"Young man," one of them said, "we can't wait forever. We have other matters to attend to."

"Please, *domini*. I'm sure that my friend and that criminal will emerge from this door shortly."

"Sorry, Son," the other watchman said, "we really don't have all day. We're wasting our time here while crimes are being committed in other parts of the city."

"You mentioned knowing where they'd be heading," the first officer said, watching my desperation, "so if you do see them leaving, you know where to find us."

"Also," the second officer added, "don't try to confront them alone. From what you said, these are dangerous thugs, and you'll be no match for them if they are determined to take your friend."

"Which is why you should have never attempted anything like this," the first officer remarked.

With all the pain in my heart, I had to let them go, finding myself in agreement with them more than ever about what a terrible idea this had been. I should have never allowed Basileus to talk me into it. My insides churned with worry. What if that evil man had forced Basileus to have sex inside the baths? No, that wouldn't be possible with so many people around. Most likely, the plan had failed, and Albus hadn't paid attention to him. At least, that's what I hoped.

Helpless, I sat on the sidewalk as I awaited the conclusion of this stupid adventure. The worst part was how I would tell Renatus, who would surely be furious with me.

Suddenly what I had been waiting for appeared before my eyes; Albus came out the back door, restraining Basileus by twisting his arm and covering his mouth.

A carriage came out of nowhere, and Albus forced Basileus inside, just as he had done to me. The nightmare was repeating itself, all because of the foolish recklessness of two boys driven by a misguided sense of justice. I should have never been so weak as to let the watchmen leave. Sneaking away to avoid attracting the attention of the criminals, I ran to the *vigiles* post in the forum and asked for help. One of the men arranged a vehicle and enlisted two additional officers, and we set off in pursuit. Within a few minutes, we reached the hideout—already secured from the inside—with the criminals' coach parked outside.

"Open up!" one of the men shouted, pounding on the door. "These are the *vigiles* of Pompeii. Open up or we'll tear it down!"

Hearing no response, the officers made good on their word and we all rushed inside. We called Albus's and Basileus's names as we ran through the halls. Faint cries for help emanated as we climbed the stairs to the second floor. Malnourished boys huddled in the corners of the rooms as the *vigiles* kicked open the doors.

"This is enough evidence to convict that man," one of them said.

"Yes, but we still have to save my friend."

As we returned to the hallways, we were attacked by two of Albus's henchmen, which were promptly stabbed by the adept *vigiles*. We opened several more doors until we reached the last one in the row. The room struck immediately as familiar; it was the same place where I had been held captive. Albus was standing inside, holding Basileus with a knife to his throat.

"Back off or I'll kill this boy!"

We all stood still.

"There is no way out for you, Albus," I said. "Release my friend now!"

"I know of your hatred for me, but consider whether your vengeance is worth your friend's blood. If I end up rotting in a cell, you'll have to live with the guilt of letting your friend die for your whims."

"Don't listen to him," Basileus uttered from beneath the heavy hand covering his mouth.

"Alright. We'll let you go. But release my friend right now. I promise to forget about all this."

"Then ask these men to leave."

I nodded to them.

"I'll let your friend go, you little troublemaker. But I'll tear your world apart if you dare to act against me."

"And how exactly are you going to do that?"

"I will reveal to the world that your father is one of my top clients."

His words chilled my blood. And though Albus had no means to prove his claim, I believed him. How naive I had been to think that my father had never satisfied his same-sex appetites, and in such a despicable manner. It wasn't difficult for me to make up my mind. I would feign that his words had coerced me into inaction, but as soon as he freed Basileus I would ensure his capture. I didn't care if he sank my father and my family's reputation in the process.

Basileus, however, took advantage of the distraction and drew a dagger from a small pocket in his tunic. Exerting visible effort, he managed to stab Albus in the abdomen, causing him to loosen his grip. The large man collapsed to the floor, clutching his belly. Basileus then stabbed him again and again before I could intervene.

"No, Basileus, no!"

The *vigiles*, who had been waiting outside, heard the commotion and rushed in as Albus lay lifeless on the ground, surrounded by a pool of blood.

At night, after Basileus and I had cleaned up, we brought chairs into the atrium of Eusebius's *domus* and were engaged in earnest conversation with Eusebius, Gaia, and Caecilia when we heard a knock on the door. Gaia got up to open it. Renatus appeared.

"They're here," she said to her son in a low voice.

Renatus entered the atrium with an expression that mixed incredulity and concern. I stood up to face him.

"Please don't get angry," I said, placing a hand on his chest. "I'm going to explain everything—"

"Those words already made me angry. Let me guess, you were outside goofing off with your friend, while we were worried about you? I've been searching for you everywhere for hours."

"I'm sorry. I'm really sorry. But it's not what you're thinking."

"It's really not at all what you're thinking, Son," Gaia said, wearing the grimmest expression I'd ever seen on her face. "Sit down with us and listen."

I recounted the story that Basileus and I had already shared with the rest of the family.

Renatus's face contorted with rage. "So, you've been trying to catch a dangerous criminal on your own, without informing any of us about it?" He stood up and knocked the chair with a swipe.

"I'm sorry, it's all my fault," Basileus said. "It was me who persuaded Lucius to rush headlong."

"But you let yourself be persuaded," Renatus said to me, ignoring Basileus and grabbing me by the collar.

"Son, please calm down," Eusebius intervened, rising, and moving toward Renatus. "We've been lecturing these boys for hours already. You don't know how distressed and embarrassed they were when they arrived. They were all covered in blood and trembling. Show a little compassion, please."

Renatus released his grip on me and paced the room.

"At least the scoundrel is dead," Caecilia said, "and those poor boys were rescued by the *vigiles*."

"I'm not saying it wasn't a good thing to put an end to that monster's life. What infuriates me is that you didn't trust us enough to mention that you had found Albus at that party."

"I'm sorry. I'm really sorry, Renatus," I said, rushing to hug him. "Will you forgive me, please?"

He didn't say a word but hugged me back.

"All of this has been really upsetting," Gaia said.

"And we even made you miss the theatrical performance," Basileus said.

"Not really," Gaia replied. "We can still catch it tomorrow, if you want."

We all looked at her in disbelief.

The next day, we were in fact ready to attend the play. Gaia had spent the morning trying to convince me that the performance was a necessary distraction from yesterday's gruesome events, but only after much prodding did she get me to agree. I wasn't in the mood for comedy, not so much because I had seen a man killed but because Albus's terrible revelation about my father still echoed in my mind.

We arrived early at the large theater to secure seats near the stage in the *media* section. The venue filled up quickly; some five thousand people were about to witness a delightful mockery of the gods. Everyone indulged in the excitement, relishing the snacks they had bought at the entrance, but I remained oblivious to the cheerful atmosphere.

Should I report my father to the authorities or simply let go of the whole matter? Albus's operations had been dismantled, so my father probably wouldn't have captive boys readily available, but what if he attempted it again? Surely Albus wasn't the only criminal in that shameful business. I didn't even know if my father traveled all the way to Pompeii to procure those boys or if Albus's operations extended to Neapolis. Considering that he had attended that party at the villa, the latter seemed more likely.

How many of those wealthy men would be involved in the business? Perhaps the ones who were touching those slaves while they groomed them. The whole thing turned my stomach—the fact that my father was part of it was unforgivable.

How was I going to tell my mother? Because I was going to tell her. She needed to know once and for all what a vile man she had been married to all these years. Doubts about my father's culpability began to assail my mind, though. What if Albus had only said that to try to save himself?

My head throbbed from going over the facts again and again, but then something came to me: the boys. The rescued boys might identify him as an offender. But if they refrained from accusing him—either because he was innocent or because they were afraid—my whole world would crumble nonetheless, as my father would never forgive me for subjecting him to a trial.

Finally, the director of the company comes on stage, and I do my best to pay attention to what's happening in front of me.

"*Salve dominarum et iudices!*" he says in a strong Greek accent. "Thank you very much for gracing us with your presence this evening. Today, we bring to you a comedy that pokes a little fun at, you know, those mighty beings living up there," he says, pointing to the sky.

A few laughs echo from the audience.

"Our central characters are: Philonous, a witty philosopher, and Dikaiopolis, an ordinary man. The rest, I believe you will recognize," he says, winking.

More laughter follows.

"People of Pompeii, to you I present: 'The Last Laugh of the Gods!'"

A roar of applause ensues. The chorus graces the stage, dressed as merchants and ordinary street people. As soon as the applause subsides, they begin reciting their lines.

"Oh, woe to us, the world's demise!

The gods above must tell us why!

The sky is falling, the earth does shake,

It seems our doom is hard to fake!"

Philonous makes his entrance, clad as an old man with a long white beard, wearing a himation over his tunic and holding a scroll.

"Hark, good people! Lend an ear,

I've read these scrolls; have no fear.

The end's upon us, that much is clear,

But, oh, how the gods themselves do jeer!"

Now Dikaiopolis, a younger man, enters the stage. He's wearing a plain, ragged, brown tunic and a short black beard.

"What nonsense is this you bring?

The end of the world? It's a terrible thing!

But why would the gods, so grand and divine,

Laugh at our fate in such a fine time?"

Philonous smirks.

"The gods above, in their lofty halls,

Are simply staging cosmic pratfalls.

For all their power and godly feats,

They've found our folly truly sweet!"

Annoyed, Juno descends from a staircase, adorned in a sumptuous stola.

"What's this I hear, you impertinent sage?

Daring to mock the gods in this age?

We may play tricks, but make no mistake,
We hold the fate of mankind at stake!"
Apollo now makes his entrance mounted on a white horse adorned with gold fittings.
"Indeed, mortal, you jest too far,
To make light of a celestial star.
Our whims may dance in the cosmic ballet,
But remember, we giveth and taketh away!"
Dikaiopolis says to Philonous, trembling:
"We've angered the gods! What shall we do?
To face their wrath, there's naught we can construe."
Philonous replies:
"Fear not, my friend, we'll stand our ground,
For laughter is the finest defense we've found.
Let the gods have their cosmic jest,
But we'll enjoy life, at its best!"
He delivers the last line while looking at the audience, who responds with enthusiastic cheers.
Jupiter, looking amused, descends from the same staircase as his wife.
"You mortals are a curious lot,
To jest and jest, with courage sought.
We'll spare you, for your wit is bright,
But heed our lessons, both day and night!"
Minerva rushes to the stage with a smile.
"In humor there's wisdom, that's true,
So, laugh with us, for we laugh with you.
The end of the world, a jest so grand,
Let's hope in laughter, you'll all withstand!"

Now Bacchus appears, carrying a wine goblet.
"To wine, to laughter, let's raise a toast,
For in mirth, our troubles are engrossed.
The world may end, but we'll go down,
With laughter echoing through the town!"
The audience erupts in cheers and applause.
The chorus chants:
"Oh, gods, we thank you for this grace,
For sparing us in this funny embrace.
But wait, there's one, who hasn't spoken yet,
Let us now hear, what Vulcan has to say!"

As Vulcan made his entrance, wielding a hammer and a torch, a great rumble shook the ground. Terrified screams filled the air. A subsequent roar, even louder, sent people fleeing from the theater, causing them to stumble over each other in their haste. We remained seated, waiting for the commotion to end, but a third shock compelled us to join the rush for the exits. The stunned theater company lingered on stage for a few more minutes before disappearing backstage. Outside, we sprinted toward the forum, aiming for an open space, steering clear of the shaking walls.

"It seems that the play did anger the gods," Basileus said.

"At least Vulcan," Caecilia said. "He didn't take it as lightly as the rest."

"What a remarkable coincidence," Eusebius chimed in.

"Do you really think it's just a coincidence?" Caecilia asked.

"It's just that, dear," Gaia said to her, taking her by the hand. "Just a coincidence. Let's go home for dinner. This was more thrilling than I anticipated."

27

The following morning, the talk of the town was the infamous performance of the theater company, which had now been expelled and forbidden to perform in Pompeii ever again. I strolled through the city center with the family to assess the aftermath of the earthquake. Some residences were reduced to rubble, prominent columns displayed significant cracks, and numerous statues lay shattered on the ground.

As we walked past one of the still-intact fountains, Caecilia reached into the water. "Ouch! By Vulcan! It's scalding hot!"

Slowly I moved my hand closer to the floating vapor. "You're right," I said, retracting my hand away as soon as my fingertips sensed the boiling liquid. "It's like a hot spring."

"It also has a peculiar smell … like sulfur," Basileus said.

"This is going to stir up people's superstitions…" Gaia said. "It's not good at all."

"But are you really sure this has nothing to do with Vulcan?" Caecilia asked. "I respect your beliefs, but I'm not convinced that we can entirely dismiss the involvement of the gods."

"There has to be a purely natural explanation for this," Renatus said. "We just don't know it yet. But one day, naturalists and philosophers will unravel the mystery."

"Where are all those people going?" Caecilia asked, pointing to a bustling group moving down the street.

"To pray to Vulcan," Eusebius replied. "The Vulcanalia festivities were already scheduled to start today, but, as Gaia mentioned, the recent events have heightened people's superstitions, so it's likely to be even more crowded this time."

"Can we join?" Caecilia suggested. "I'd feel more at ease if I could at least offer a prayer to help appease the god."

"I'm curious to see what it's all about as well," I said. "Would you like to come with us?"

"Nah, youngsters," Gaia said, "we're a bit too old for that. And you know we don't believe in those things anyway. You can go; it's good to satisfy one's curiosity and find some peace of mind, if that's what you're looking for."

"I'm going with them, Mom," Renatus said.

Gaia nodded with a smile. "Alright, Eusebius and I will go home."

The four of us walked through the busy streets, where numerous bonfires had already been set up in front of houses and shops. Some individuals were tossing sacrificed fishes and small land animals onto the fires, while others offering wheat and small cakes.

After some time, we arrived at the temple, where a large crowd had already assembled. We maneuvered through the gathering, pushing our way inside, where an immense bull had been brought for sacrifice in front of Vulcan's sacred fire. The priest chanted words of worship as he slit the throat of the poor beast, splashing the altar with its blood. At that moment, a sweaty, ragged-looking man with a disgruntled expression approached us.

"What are you atheists doing here? Don't think we don't know what kind of people your parents are," he said, pointing to Renatus. "You unbelievers have enraged the gods and provoked the wrath of Vulcan!" He spat on the floor before us. "Now, get out of here, before we give you the beating you deserve. Get out!"

A group of people formed around us, hurling menacing insults. We ran out into the street.

"Did you manage to offer your prayer?" I asked Caecilia.

"No, but if what that man claimed is true, I doubt Vulcan would entertain a prayer from an atheist like me," she said with a chuckle.

That brought me satisfaction. Perhaps this experience would help Caecilia grasp our perspective. "See?" I said to her. "I've told you how religion breeds violence. Nothing good comes out of superstitious beliefs. Let's leave them alone with their follies and make the most of our day."

"Just one final request, and I assure you I'll drop this whole matter," Caecilia said. "Can we visit a seer? It would make me feel better to have confirmation that nothing untoward will happen."

Renatus shrugged.

"Besides," Caecilia said to me, "you've been having these strange dreams about Mount Vesuvius; it wouldn't hurt to find out what they signify. You always find yourself in the midst of an earthquake, right?"

"That's true," I replied.

"It should be fun," Basileus chimed in. "Plus, I've never been to one, so I'm really curious."

We strolled along the street where seers and fortune tellers had their posts and settled on one that advertised being able to both interpret dreams and predict future events. It was a squeezed space permeated by the potent aroma of myrrh. Inside, a diminutive elderly woman with cataract-clouded eyes, her long hair braided with ribbons, sat in lotus position on a rectangular oriental rug with straw baskets on either side. In front of her was a small fire with an iron griddle.

"Come on in," she said in a sharp, high-pitched voice with a foreign accent, as she beckoned to us with her tiny hand. "You're fortunate to be in the presence of Petrea's finest sibyl, as my stay in Pompeii will be very short. What can I do for you today?"

"I have a recurrent dream that I would like you to interpret," I said. "I have reasons to believe it is related to yesterday's earthquake."

"That's very good, young man, you've come to the right place. Toss twenty sesterces into the basket and recount your dream in detail, sparing no aspect," she hissed.

I narrated the vision of walking barefoot on soil atop Mount Vesuvius, consistently witnessing Renatus trapped in an earthquake, and my inability to aid his escape.

"There's nothing to worry about, young man. It just goes to show a profound concern for your friend," she said, squinting. "I presume there is a strong bond between the two of you, am I right?"

"Yes, there is." I couldn't lie if I wanted an accurate interpretation, but I hoped she could grasp the essence of our connection without specifics. *If she's a good seer, she should be able to "see" that.*

"I understand completely," she said with a knowing smile. "Was your friend in any form of peril?"

"Yes, he was abducted. The dreams began when we were attempting to locate him."

"And they persisted even after you found him?"

"Exactly. That's what struck me as strange. It's one of the reasons we suspect they might be linked to yesterday's occurrences. We want to discern whether this is not a forecast of some impending calamity."

"For that, we'll have to consult the serpents," she said, groping for one of the baskets on her left, and extracting from it a smooth, small green snake with black bands along the body.

The reptile seemed tame, as it made no attempt to bite her, even though it hadn't been defanged. The woman caressed it to assure its trust; then, with a sudden motion, gripped it by the neck and strangled it. The snake wriggled for a brief moment before becoming motionless. The seer severed its head with a sharp knife, made a superficial incision in its belly, and peeled off the poor vermin's skin.

She cut the body into small pieces and threw them one by one onto the griddle, inhaling the vapors. She began to speak in whispers, in a language unknown to us. Then she said in full voice, "I see the city... Pompeii... I see the city... Many people walking through its streets..."

Then everything will be alright.

The pitch and volume of her voice increased, becoming a terrifying shriek.

"People wearing strange clothes, speaking in foreign tongues... People—" She halted abruptly, her face contorted in fear. "Destruction... Destruction! Roofs vanished, columns in ruins!" She panted heavily. "Houses exposed, temples obliterated, no remnants of the sacred or the holy, everything has disappeared, everything is gone! Ahhh!"

Her shriek grew to an unbearable volume, making us cover our ears.

"Strange people smiling at rectangular mirrors, pointing them at the ruins... Men wearing *bracae* like the Persians; women... impudent women showing their arms, legs, and cleavage... They all seem happy... very happy... They relish in the destruction! They're not Romans! Not Romans!"

She desperately covered her ears. "Ahhh, that music! That horrible music!"

We looked at each other in astonishment.

"Two men with long hair, playing strange lutes tied to big boxes with ropes... Another man, beating an assemble of drums like a madman... A fourth man, seated at a large table with white teeth, pressing them and producing the most dreadful sounds! They sing to sticks with round edges. They are alone! Alone in the amphitheater. No other people around. Oh, that sound! That horrible sound! Stop, stop!"

She snapped out of the trance, drenched in sweat. She gazed at us, seemingly unable to recall why we were there.

"Thank you," Caecilia said, dropping twenty more sesterces in her basket. "That's all we needed to know."

We walked out of the shop, leaving the bewildered woman behind.

"What was all that?" Basileus asked. "What does it even have to do with Lucius's dream?"

"Let's find a quiet place to sit down and discuss it," Caecilia said.

"Let's go to my dad's library," Renatus suggested.

We arrived a few minutes later and arranged chairs around Eusebius's desk.

"Alright, let's review the facts," I said.

"All that destruction doesn't seem related to your dreams," Basileus said.

Renatus got up and started browsing the shelves.

"Or with the earthquake, for that matter," I added. "It sounded more like devastation of war, especially with foreign people walking around. And what about those clothes she described? Men in *bracae*? Does that mean the Persians are going to conquer us?"

"The question is, why did she experience that vision just now when we inquired about the dream?" Caecilia pondered. "There must be a connection."

"Let's get things straight," I said. "In my dreams, there's always an earthquake that I'm trying to rescue Renatus from. We're at the top of Mount Vesuvius, and the earth feels intensely hot, as if the mountain itself is filled with wrath."

"Just like Vulcan yesterday during the play," Basileus said.

"So, there are two things in common," I continued. "The apparent fury of Vulcan, and an earthquake."

"Then, she witnessed the city in ruins, roofs vanished, houses toppled..." Caecilia remarked. "That could be the continuation of your dream."

"Look," Renatus said, unfurling two scrolls on the desk. "I recalled that Mount Vesuvius was mentioned in some of these books. And I found it," he said, indicating a verse on one of the papyri. "This is 'Geographica' by Strabo. Take a look at this passage: *'Above these places is Mount Vesuvius ... ash-colored to the eye, cavernous hollows appear formed of blackened stones, looking as if they had been subjected to the action of fire. From this we may infer that the place was formerly in a burning state with live craters, which however became extinguished on the failing of the fuel.'*"

"What?" I said.

"And now, look at this," he said, pointing to the other scroll. "*'It is no less mentioned that in ancient times fires grew and abounded under Mount Vesuvius, and from thence spewed out flames around the fields.'* This is what Vitruvius says."

"Then there is some truth to my dream. Mount Vesuvius is a mountain of fire?"

EVAN D. BERG

"That means there is indeed an impending loom upon us," Caecilia said. "How is it that no one is aware of this?"

"Because no one reads books," Renatus said. "Plus, these references are so old that collective memory may have forgotten that Mount Vesuvius is a timeless threat."

"The only element that doesn't align is the presence of those foreign people in the seer's visions," Basileus said. "Especially the way she depicted them, casually strolling with little mirrors in their hands and in peculiar attire."

"And what makes the least sense of all is the music she described," Caecilia said.

"It all comes down to something really bad happening to Pompeii," I concluded.

"But when?" Renatus questioned. "And what can we do to prevent it?"

"If it truly is Vulcan's fury, there's little we can do," Caecilia replied. We gazed at her inquisitively. "Don't look at me like that," she said with a grin. "I'm sorry, but I still believe in the possibility of the gods mingling in our lives."

"But even if there's nothing we can do, that doesn't mean it's the will of the gods," Renatus said. "I still believe it's simply a natural occurrence. Man is insignificant against the forces of nature."

"We could propose evacuating," I suggested.

"Yeah, as if they would believe us," Basileus remarked.

"There have already been enough signs that some of them might," I replied.

"But we don't know exactly when it will happen," Renatus said. "There was a strong earthquake seventeen years

242

ago. Mount Vesuvius didn't spit fire that time. If they leave and nothing happens, they will come after us."

"And another reason why I doubt people will believe us," Caecilia said, "is because they see Mount Vesuvius as a genius providing abundant game, timber and fertile land for wine; why would the notion that it wants to harm us even cross their minds?"

"That leads us back to Vulcan's fury," Basileus said. "Perhaps if we approach it from the superstitious side, they might believe... They're fearful; that's why they went to the temple to pray."

"I believe there's only one thing we can do," Renatus proposed. We all looked at him. "Let's follow the suggestion from the play yesterday. Just drink and enjoy our time while the world crumbles."

We burst into laughter.

"We can try," I said, though not entirely convinced. "Where should we go?"

"It's a little late for *prandium*, but do you want to see if my parents haven't eaten yet? I'm hungry with all this research," Renatus said.

We found Gaia in the kitchen bustling around with the slaves while a delightful aroma of baking bread filled the air.

"So you've returned from your religious excursion?" she asked upon seeing us. "How did it go?"

"Not very well, I'm afraid," Caecilia replied. "We were called atheists and kicked out of the temple."

"It doesn't surprise me," Gaia said with a smile. "Some religious people tend to be extremely judgmental of other people's beliefs. But now you've seen it for yourselves."

Eusebius walked into the kitchen and hugged his wife from behind.

"So you're baking *panis focacius*, honey?"

"Yes," she said, turning to him and planting a small peck. "Just the way you like it, with olive oil and cheese. And roasted eggplant on the side."

"Sounds delicious," I said. " Can we join?"

"Of course, darling, you don't have to ask."

After a brief wait, we were all sitting down at the kitchen table.

"Come on, my dears," Gaia said, noting our glum expressions. "Forget about the temple; what happened there is of no importance."

"The temple isn't the only reason we're upset," I said. I signaled to Renatus to share what we had discovered.

"We read from two scrolls in the library that Vesuvius is a mountain of fire."

"So you've just found that out?" Eusebius said, taking a bite of his bread. "You need to study more, my Son."

"I recalled having read about it before. Luckily, I managed to locate the reference."

"So what's the problem?" Eusebius asked.

"Well, you've seen what has been happening since yesterday," I said, "the little quake, the boiling water in the fountains… and also my nightmares…"

"What nightmares?" Gaia asked.

I filled her in with the details of my unsettling dreams and the seer's vision.

"I agree that everything appears quite ominous," Gaia said. "But there are many aspects of Mother Nature that remain unknown to us. We don't know how atoms combine inside the earth, for example." She gazed at our unconvinced faces. "Yet, you should rejoice in the fact that we are alive today, my darlings; that's the essence of life."

"Alive today," Basileus said, "but on the brink of destruction, thanks to Mount Vesuvius."

"My mom is right," Renatus said. "We can't control what nature has in store for us. But we can control how we spend our time until then."

"Besides, worrying won't change a thing," Gaia said.

""Absolutely," Eusebius said. "Now, let's enjoy a sip of this wine. It's truly 'divine.'"

We raised our cups amid laughter.

"That's the spirit!" Gaia said.

"You're right," Basileus said. "Who knows what the future holds? Maybe Vulcan is just playing a massive prank on us."

"Prank or not, I still believe in the gods," Caecilia said. "And I sincerely hope that Vulcan has taken this with a pinch of humor."

"Well, if 'the gods' have a plan, I hope it involves blessing the soil to give us more grapes to produce this heavenly wine," Renatus said, taking another sip.

"I hear Bacchus has a plan," Gaia said, raising her goblet. "It's throwing a party for the end of the world! He's calling it the 'Doomsday Grape Bash'!"

We all burst into laughter.

"You have no idea," she continued. "He insists it's going to be a grand event to 'wine down' life on this crazy world!"

"Gaia, you're out of control today," Eusebius said with a chuckle.

"Wait, do you want to know what the grape said when it got stepped on?" Gaia asked.

"What?" we asked.

"Nothing. It just let out a little 'wine.'"

"Come on," Eusebius said, wiping away the tears of laughter.

"So shall we 'wine' until the world wobbles?" Renatus said.

"Exactly!" Gaia said. "And you know Bacchus, he's got this divine plan to turn all water into wine. It'll spare us from worrying about Vesuvius; we'll be too tipsy to notice the chaos."

"To Bacchus and his world-ending feast!" Basileus proposed, raising his goblet.

We clinked our goblets in a precious moment of laughter that obliterated the uncertainty of the future.

A couple of hours later, Gaia had retired to tend to her plants, and Eusebius to his *tablinum*. We remained in the kitchen, polishing off another amphora of wine.

"What do you want to do now?" I asked.

"Why don't we go to the baths?" Renatus suggested.

"No, we can't take Caecilia there," I said, "I'm certain you don't want to go to the ladies' section by yourself."

"You can go; I can help Gaia with her gardening," Caecilia offered.

"I'll stay too," Basileus said.

"That's fine by me," Renatus said. "Shall we go, Lucius?"

I headed for the door with Renatus, a little uncomfortable about leaving Caecilia with Basileus. Was I jealous? Certainly not. In fact, I was relieved. Fortunately, Caecilia harbored no romantic feelings for me. So, if something developed between her and Basileus... that would complete the circle. It was a strange idea, but one that had the potential to solve everything for us. Was it inappropriate? Certainly society wouldn't understand it, but Gaia and Eusebius would, and they'd be supportive. That was all that mattered.

28

More than a little tipsy, Renatus and I walked to the Forum baths, which we had never visited before.

"There's no water," the doorkeeper informed us, "but the dry sections are open, if you're interested."

"Maybe we should try the Stabians," I whispered to Renatus.

"They don't have water either," the man clarified. "It's a city-wide problem. The water from the aqueduct is so hot that it's evaporating before reaching the baths."

Renatus and I exchanged bewildered glances. "It's alright," Renatus said, "we were mainly interested in renting a room anyway."

The amenities of these baths were decent but couldn't compare to the opulence of the Stabians. Our room was tidy, though, clearly benefiting from extra attention from the housekeepers due to the low turnout caused by the water problem. I sprawled on the bed, and Renatus promptly began to remove his tunic.

"You know, love," I murmured, caressing his chest, "with everything that's been happening, I need some genuine relaxation. And there's only one thing that's going to do it for me this time."

"Oh, I know," he said with a smirk. "You naughty boy. I was actually going to suggest tantric myself."

"Then, let's make the room a little cozier."

I left and returned shortly with two lit candles, a stick of incense, and a small jar. I ignited the incense and placed it in a holder on the wall.

"Move the mattress to the floor." I positioned the candles on each side. "I also brought this," I said, showing him the jar with scented oil.

"You've thought of everything."

I winked. I sat down on the mat and asked him to sit in front of me.

"Where did you learn this?"

"At the retreat."

He looked at me with reproachful eyes.

"Don't look at me like that. I didn't go as far as making love with anyone. I would only do it with you."

"I know, silly. But even if you had been intimate with other men, only with me can you truly make love." He smiled and took my hands. "Even though you now have more knowledge about these arts, I still have more experience than you, so I'll be your guide."

"Fine," I said with a smile.

"But stop me if I go too far. To have a true tantric experience, we have to try to have multiple orgasms while retaining the seed. I know it sounds ambitious, but I'm all for it and I know you are too."

We began in the nude, adopting the same lotus position that Basileus and I had used in the retreat. We felt each other's heartbeats, exchanging smiles as we synchronized our breathing, the deep connection that already existed between Renatus and me coming to the surface.

Following this brief warm-up, he had me lie on my back with my head on a pillow. Leaning toward me, our fingers intertwined, he gently touched my lips with his. The harmony of our bodies resonated within me.

Sliding down, he gently stroked my chest with his incipient beard, and my sides with his expert hands; I could do nothing but surrender to his touch. He lingered on my belly, planting kisses along my treasure trail. Like a feather's brush, he traversed delicately between my thighs, his touch eliciting a delightful shiver.

He returned to my upper body, rubbing his face on my neck and cheeks, and gently nibbling my earlobe. He moved down my pecs toward my nipples, sucking them gently as he smiled mischievously at me. The amalgamation of pleasure and pain sent a powerful sensation rippling through my body. Recognizing the intensity of my response, he released my throbbing nipples—now as erect as my cock—and pleasured them with soothing licks.

He retrieved some oil from the jar, spreading it across his hands. The warmth of his touch as he cupped my testicles further invigorated my arousal. Moving to the tip of my cock, he retracted the foreskin, rolling his fingers over the moist glans. My legs arched and my toes curled as a response to the powerful stimulation.

My male organ now became the sole focus of his attention. He began by licking the frenulum as his eyes locked onto mine. He kissed the head of the cock and sucked it like a juicy fruit, licking the clear syrup that trickled from it. By the time he went all the way down on my shaft my body was already on the verge of ecstasy, so I had to quickly recall how to perform the great aspiration to move the orgasm from my groin to my head. I patted him, signaling him to stop. He performed the tapping motion on my cock, guided by the intensity of my moans, and when he sensed that I was getting close, he stopped and distracted me by touching my balls and lightly pressing my perineum. He teased my hole a bit, but the moment for full exploration had not yet arrived.

He went back to sucking my cock a few more times, and masturbated it with the pumping motion in between, pausing to caress my balls when I told him I was close. After a while, he had learned to read me so well that he stopped the stimulation exactly when I was on the verge of cumming, as if he could feel the sensations in my body. Then he pumped me so hard that I felt the tingle of impending orgasm.

"I'm cumming, I'm cumming!"

He throttled the base of my cock and balls and pressed hard on my perineum with two fingers, and I did my part by firmly squeezing my hole and rhythmically moving my buttocks upward while performing the great aspiration. Under normal conditions, a strong stream of cum would have already been expelled from my penis, but as this path was sealed by his grip, the orgasmic energy had nowhere to go but up my spine and into my head.

The climax far surpassed that of my previous solo experience. With Renatus blocking my exit, I found a deeper sense of relaxation, allowing myself to surrender entirely to the pleasure. Closing my eyes, peculiar circles of color manifested and vanished within the recesses of my mind. The energy coursing through my body enveloped me in warmth and delight. It took some time for my breathing to return to normal after descending from the heightened state. Eventually, I opened my eyes to find Renatus smiling at me, gradually loosening his hold on my cock and balls.

"What was that?" I whispered.

"Just the beginning."

I looked down and confirmed than not a drop of cum had leaked out of my cock.

"Are you tired?"

"No, I feel incredible; this was far more intense than when I had done it on my own."

"That's because I'm here with you, love." He gave me a peck and lay beside me. "I'm glad you're not tired because there's still much more to come."

After cuddling for a while, Renatus had me lie on my back again, my flaccid penis resting on one side, still recovering from the intense excitement it had endured. He rubbed his face on my belly, where much of the orgasmic energy still lingered, and caressed my arms and chest, moving upward until his face was next to mine. He kissed me passionately while stroking my chest and buttocks. In return, I ran my hands over his back and pulled him closer until we melded in a warm embrace. He sucked my lips as his hand playfully fondled my cock and balls, my cock eagerly responding to his touch.

He rose to reach for a little oil, which he spread on my hole, allowing his fingers to frolic around it. He gradually inserted one of them, gently stretching my orifice and playing with its folds as he sensed my response. A few minutes later, I was relaxed enough to receive a second finger. The pleasure of the stretching escalated, merging with the remnants of the orgasm I had just had. When I least expected it, a third finger went in, eliciting moaning from me.

"Are you alright?"

"Yes, just be gentle, please."

He continued to push his fingers into me, discovering an area inside that gave me an intense surge of pleasure.

"Right there, right there, ahh!"

"Now I know where your spot is, I'll be sure to touch it when I enter you fully."

I was burning inside, seething with desire for his penetration.

He got up and knelt in front of me, as I continued to lie face up on the mattress. He pulled another pillow from the bed and placed it under my buttocks. He played a little with his now iron-hard cock, rubbing its head against my balls, running it down the perineum, teasing my hole making it suck his moist glans.

"Please, I'm yearning for you."

He entered me barely an inch, then an inch more, then withdrew, keeping my hole open with the head of his cock.

"Ahh, do it again, please."

He repeated the motion in a slow and controlled manner, initiating a pattern that was taking me to the heavens once again. Moving his cock in circles, he looked for my spot. Gazing at me with a smile, he entwined our fingers. *This is love.*

"Ahh, yes, you found it. Right there, love, right there."

He hit my spot repeatedly, varying speed, depth, angle, and intensity.

"Do you like it, love?"

"Yes, keep going, please."

He has never made love to me like this.

He pushed my legs down and lifted my ass more as he leaned over me, bouncing his pelvis like a rider's ass on a trotting horse. He pushed in a little further, hitting a second sensitive part that felt like a small pouch.

"Ahh, Renatus, you've hit another spot." My groin sent waves of pleasure throughout my body.

"Jerk off and control the movements when you start to feel the orgasmic tingling. This will be very intense."

I followed his directions and masturbated with the pumping motion first to regain my hard on, then tapped my penis to feel just the right amount of orgasmic tingle without erupting.

"I'm getting close," I warned him.

"I'm getting close too," he said, pulling out a little without removing his cock completely from my hole, and taking deep breaths to control his own orgasm.

"I'm already releasing a lot of precum," he said. "I don't know if we'll reach the top at the same time."

"We can try."

He used profound motions to thrust himself back inside, his cock sliding delightfully into my passage, aided by the additional lubrication of his precum. My cock bounced on my stomach and leaked profusely. I could only explain my sensations as a flock of seagulls playing with the waves of a sea of desire that had surged within me.

His circular movements widened, exploiting the sensitivity of my anus to the fullest, sending waves of heat through my body up to my head. It was an intoxication more powerful than that of wine, incense, and herbs combined. The pleasure made me feel weak and revitalized at the same time.

"I'm at the top of the mountain, love, I don't know if I can take much more."

"Then stop touching yourself a little."

I let go of my penis and the excitement subsided a bit. However, my anus began to throb involuntarily with his cock inside, as it continued to send signals to the rest of my body that orgasm was imminent.

"Now you know what to do," he said, slowing down and looking at my ecstatic expression. "Hold your dick and balls tight, while you squeeze my cock hard with your hole. Take deep breaths and focus on making the pleasure go up your body and away from your genitals."

"I'll try," I said, panting.

"Do you want me to resume pounding you?"

"Yes, please."

He fucked me hard, going all the way at full speed. I masturbated vigorously, only stopping at the moment when release felt imminent. I choked my cock to keep it from cumming. He continued to pound me and hit my second spot again. My orgasm was so intense that if I hadn't had my hand on my cock I would have cum all over. But instead, my body disintegrated into an infinite mass of pleasure, morphing into a river of fire cascading onto the sun.

I lost all sense of time and space; I even forgot that Renatus was inside me. I was no longer myself; I became one with the universe—akin to the wind, stars, moon, and sea—a god among gods. Supreme happiness swept over me.

When I regained earthly consciousness, Renatus, drenched in sweat, was resting on me, his body an extension of mine. *There will no longer be a "he and I"; now he is me, and I am him.*

29

Reality returned to me in the guise of another workday. I had become more proficient in the legal profession, and now, with the sweet memory of the tantric experience with Renatus, the hours of the day slipped away effortlessly.

Yet, an uneasy concern lingered: broaching with my mother the dreadful truth about my father. Despite my apprehension, I seized the opportunity to meet with her alone during my father's absence for a court session.

She gasped, putting her hand to her chest as she saw me enter the kitchen. "Oh Lucius, you startled me! I'm preparing the dough for the sweet bread you like so much."

Drawing closer, I placed my hands on her shoulders.

"Why have you come to the kitchen? It's no place for a man."

"I need to talk to you about something. Can we go to the *tablinum*?"

A shadow crossed her face, signaling her anticipation of a challenging conversation. She wiped her hands, took off her apron, and joined me. Upon entering the *tablinum*, we sat at my desk.

"What is it, Lucius? Shouldn't your father be present?"

"No. It's something I must discuss with you first before confronting my father."

"Confronting?" Her face now showed an anxious expression.

I took a deep breath. "I've discovered things about Father that are… very unsettling."

She remained silent.

"It's a long story, Mother. I'll try to make it as short as possible. I was kidnapped during my time in Pompeii."

"Are you admitting that those people you so vehemently defended had in fact kidnapped you? Did they threaten you? You should have told us from the start, and your father would have had them prosecuted—"

"No, Mother, it's nothing like that. I was kidnapped one day at the baths. I'm ashamed to admit it, but the criminals intended to use me as a sex slave. Fortunately, I managed to find a way to escape… but other boys weren't as fortunate."

"And how does this relate to your father?" Her face was now transfixed in terror.

"I encountered the man who kidnapped me at Pompeius's party. We devised a trap for the authorities apprehend him, but things went terribly wrong, and he was fatally wounded. Before he died, though… he revealed to me that my father was a client of his gang."

"You can't possibly believe that. It's all a lie, a vicious lie!"

"I'm not so sure, Mother. You acknowledged that my father's inclinations are similar to mine. I fear he's been indulging his desires in the most repugnant manner."

"I can't believe you're saying such things, Lucius." She rose. "How dare you claim that your father, the honorable Lucius Cornelius Successianus, is involved with criminals of such heinous kind."

"That's why I talked to you first." I approached her. Gripping her arms, I compelled her to look at me. "Do you swear by the gods that you were unaware of this?"

She stared at me with frantic eyes.

"So you knew. How could you tolerate it?" I blurted out, releasing her. "I can't believe it. What kind of monsters are you?"

"The kind of monsters to raise you and give you everything!"

"Then I don't want any of it!"

"Tell me, what choice did I have? Divorcing him would have been a scandal. No other man would have wanted to marry me. Besides, he would have taken you away. I would have lost you, everything I have in this world." She drew closer to me, but I rejected her.

"Does he know that you know?"

"Of course. I've told you before; there are no secrets between us."

"Am I really his son, Mother? Don't lie."

Her eyes filled with tears. "Yes, Lucius. You are his flesh and blood. I would never deceive you. He lay with me just one time, and that solitary occasion was enough to conceive you. I had prayed to Juno so fervently, hoping that when I could finally persuade him to grant me that favor, she would be gracious enough to bless me with a son, and she did. She gave you to me."

"I can't believe you've turned the blind eye all these years. Those boys were slaves, Mother. Held against their will to provide sick pleasure to perverted men. Couldn't my father have gone to the baths or at least procure himself with a prostitute from the streets?"

"He couldn't risk being seen in public. We have a reputation to look after. Can you imagine the social ridicule if he had been exposed?"

"What about their suffering?"

"What about my suffering? Do you think I haven't suffered all these years, knowing what I know? But I kept quiet. All for the greater good, to save my marriage and to protect you."

"You didn't have to protect me at that cost. I'll put an end to it. I will report him to the authorities," I declared, heading for the door.

"You have no proof!"

"I'm confident the boys who were liberated after my kidnapper's demise will be able to identify him when I bring him to trial."

"You will not take such action." She reached for me and tugged at my robe. "If your father sets foot in jail," she declared in a chilling tone, "I'll kill myself. I won't live to see you bring disgrace to your own family."

"You've completely lost your mind!"

"You've been warned. If you're willing to bear the guilt of causing your own mother's death, proceed! Continue with your reckless actions."

I took to the street with no clear direction.

Returning home in the evening, still reeling from my mother's stance, I was met in the atrium by a distressed Caecilia, along with Renatus.

"Lucius, I'm relieved you're back," she said, embracing me. "Something terrible has happened."

More bad news—just what I needed. "What is it?"

"Bar the door."

I followed her directive and returned to the atrium.

"I ventured out of the house to get groceries," Renatus began.

"But love, you know that's really dangerous."

"I'm sorry," he said, looking embarrassed. "I got tired of being cooped up inside." He paused. "And now you can guess what happened."

"Did one of my father's men spot you?"

He nodded. "I'm not entirely sure, but judging by the way he stared at me, it's possible he recognized me."

"Were you followed?"

"I don't know. I did my best trying to act casual, and I came home through one of the *insulae* to try to lose anyone who might be following me."

"You did well," I said. "But this changes things."

"This changes everything," Caecilia said. "We can anticipate your father scrutinizing our house any moment now."

"He probably doesn't know yet. He was in court all day. I'm not sure whether he's returned home by now."

"If it was indeed one of your father's men who saw Renatus, he will surely wait for him to get home to break the news.

"Still, I don't think—" My words were cut short by loud banging on the door.

"Lucius!" a furious voice, unmistakably my father's, bellowed from outside. "Open the door! Open up, immediately!"

"What do we do now?" Caecilia hissed.

Ramose, the slave we had rescued from Pompeius, approached. "May the masters forgive me for overhearing," he said, casting his eyes to the floor. "I dare interrupt now because I can propose a solution." We looked at each other. "Escape out the back, I'll meet the master's father at the front and distract him and his men to buy you time to get away."

"But we can't abandon you here, Ramose," Caecilia protested. "We don't know what he might do to all of you when he discovers that we're gone."

"The masters once saved me, and now it's my turn to reciprocate. Besides, if I and the other slaves play our part well, there's a chance to earn his mercy, which, with all due respect, the masters won't receive. This is the only way, *domina*, please accept my solution."

Caecilia glanced at me, and I nodded.

"Go now!" Ramose insisted, to the sound of someone kicking the door.

She took his face in her hands and kissed him on the cheek. "May your gods bless you, Ramose." He bowed slightly.

Caecilia, Renatus, and I hurried to the back door as Ramose informed my father that I had a headache, and we had retired early to our quarters, while my father shouted my name along with profanities. After running a few blocks and making sure we weren't being followed, we stopped in a dark alley to gather our thoughts.

"What are we going to do?" Caecilia asked. "This was certainly not part of the plan."

"It's a disaster," I said, running my hands through my hair. "And what happened with Renatus isn't the only problem," I confessed to their worried faces. "I told my mother of my intention to have my father arrested for his involvement with a sex trafficking ring."

"What are you talking about?" Caecilia asked with a frowning face.

"Before dying, Albus revealed that my father was one of his clients."

Caecilia and Renatus stared at me with wild eyes.

"I had intended to share this with you, but I needed to confront my mother first," I said, looking at them. "And not only did she know everything, but she threatened to take her own life if I acted against him. She cynically admitted that there are no secrets between them, so I'm sure she told him all about it."

"Is that why you came home so late?" Caecilia asked.

"Yes. I went out for a walk, hoping it would clear my thoughts. It didn't. And when I returned home, this happened."

"I'm so sorry, love," Renatus said, clinging to me. "I've only made things worse."

I patted his shoulder. "We must come up with a plan. But first we have to find refuge from my father's wrath."

"We can't do that in Neapolis," Caecilia said. "Everybody knows him, and they'll likely support him. There's only one place where we can be safe."

"Pompeii?" I asked.

"Exactly," Caecilia replied.

"But how can we leave the city at night?" I asked.

"You should know, you've already did it once," Renatus quipped.

"No time for jokes," I said, giving Renatus a disapproving look. "Besides, I didn't escape at night. I had to wait until dawn to try to hide on one of those donkey carts."

"With money, we can work something out," Caecilia said. She had been foresighted enough to grab a purse of gold as we left. "This is what's left of the dowry. It's not much, but let's make sure we put it to good use."

We emerged from the alley and stepped into the still bustling streets. The fading light of the dusty evening reminded us of the urgency to escape before the city gates shut for the night. In a race against the dimming sun, we reached the market square.

Caecilia approached an old horse dealer as he was packing up. "*Salve*. We need to rent two horses."

As weary as he looked, a last-minute business is never to be turned down—especially from seemingly well-heeled people in a hurry—so he gave us his full attention. "Have you rented horses from me before?"

"No. Just give us two of your finest specimens, but quick," Caecilia said.

The old man entered the stable and returned with two well-kept horses, one white and one pinto. "These are my two best, but they come at a premium."

"Can we leave them in Pompeii?" Caecilia asked. "We only need them for a one-way trip."

The man nodded. "Leave them at the Aureus Mane Stabulae."

The dealer's eyes widened when Caecilia handed him a handful of coins, and he quickly readied the horses, as a distant clang reminded us that there was no time to lose. We arrived just as the guards had pushed the massive doors closed.

"Wait," I said. "Please reopen the gates. We must leave the city now; we have urgent news for a relative in Pompeii."

The guards exchanged skeptical glances. "Once the gates are closed they can't be reopened," one of them said.

"What if you're criminals trying to escape?" another said with a menacing look.

"Do we look like criminals to you?" I said, gesturing for the men to look at our fine clothes. "This is not how patricians should be treated."

"We must inform the prefect of your request," the first guard declared, standing an inch away from me. "No one, regardless of their status, may leave the city once the gates are closed."

Caecilia repeated her magic trick, throwing her purse with the remaining coins in their direction. "Keep it. But open the gates now and don't tell anyone you've seen us."

The guards looked at each other and grinned. They opened the gates just enough for us to pass, as they looked in all directions. Caecilia and I mounted the white horse, and Renatus the pinto.

"We must hurry and try to reach Pompeii before nightfall," Caecilia said.

"The gates of Pompeii will be closed," Renatus said behind us. "We can stay at my dad's farm, which is halfway."

I nodded to Renatus. We spurred the horses into the open road, leaving Neapolis behind. A good night's rest would give us a clear mind to decide our next steps.

"What a delightful surprise," Gaia said the next morning, welcoming us along with Eusebius at the door. "You're just in time for *ientaculum*."

Minutes later, we were relishing a modest meal of bread, butter, and honey, made special, of course, by the warmth of their company. I felt at home again, just like that first time in their villa.

"There's much to discuss, Mom," Renatus said, chewing on his bread. "Why don't you tell them, Lucius?" He nudged me. "You're better at talking than me."

Gaia and Eusebius attentively listened to my account.

"This is quite an interesting development," Gaia said. "But you made a wise decision. You're safe here with us. We won't allow him to interfere in our lives anymore."

"I don't think we'll shake my father off so easily. He never gives up when he's set on doing something."

"But now we have a powerful weapon against him with the testimonies of those boys who could incriminate him," Eusebius said. "We can threaten him with a scandal if he dares to continue harassing you."

"Eusebius is right," Gaia said. "You have the right to do whatever it takes to start a new life, and my son needs to be free again to roam the streets," she added, taking his hand.

"I think we should also tell Basileus that we're here," Caecilia said.

I smirked at her.

Caecilia, Renatus, and I walked a bit later through the busy streets in the direction of Basileus's residence, the sun beaming brightly in the middle of the sky.

"I'm not sure if it's wise to be in the city right now," Renatus said. He sounded uncharacteristically cautious, perhaps still feeling guilty about his mishap. "What if we've been followed here?"

"I don't think my father suspects we're in Pompeii," I said.

"Where else would we be?" Renatus said. "By now, he must have turned Neapolis upside down trying to find us."

"I hope that at least the guards at the gate didn't give us away," Caecilia said.

"I'm sure Basileus will be delighted to see you," I said to Caecilia with a wink. She smirked.

A few minutes later, we reached Basileus's home. He greeted us at the door, a little surprised by our early arrival, and led us to the garden.

"In that case, you should consider making arrangements to stay here in Pompeii permanently," he said, after we had shared our problems with him. "I mean, Lucius, now that you're a married man and officially emancipated from your father's guardianship, there's little he can do to compel you to return."

"You have no idea, my friend. His power influence extends well into Pompeii. Look what he tried to do to Eusebius and Gaia."

"But he failed," Renatus pointed out. "And I'm sure his reputation suffered. I doubt he would try anything against them after that."

"He could ensure I don't find work," I said.

"Haven't you been saying that you want to be an artist?" Renatus said. "Maybe it's time you dedicate some time to your 'art.'"

I playfully punched him.

"It's kind of hot right now," Basileus said, "you want to get an ice?"

As we strolled toward our favorite honeyed ice shop, I noticed at a distance two men browsing around town.

"Look," I whispered, discreetly pointing at them. "Those are my father's *lictores*. He sent them to follow us." My friends turned to glance in their direction. "Let's walk back," I said. "Discreetly."

They heeded my advice, and we retraced our steps to Basileus's home. I didn't dare to look back, but Basileus did. "They saw us!" he warned us. "They're coming our way!"

Panic surged through me as we sprinted through the narrow streets. We weaved through alleyways, trying to lose them amid the labyrinthine maze of buildings and structures.

Breathless, I cast a few glances over my shoulder. My father's *lictores* were drawing closer, their fasces glinting in the dappled sunlight that pierced through the cramped buildings. We darted into a secluded alley, the scent of damp stone and aged wood mingling in the air. The narrow path swallowed us, providing temporary concealment. We huddled against the wall, our hearts pounding as one.

"We can't stay here long," Renatus said. "If they find us, we'll have nowhere to run."

The men remained unseen for a moment, making me think we had successfully evaded them. I signaled my friends to emerge from our respite, and we carefully made it back to the street. After walking a short distance, however, a very familiar voice behind us snapped me back to reality.

"Lucius!" my father shouted.

We had just started to run again when a blast, louder than anything I had ever heard in my life, brought us to an abrupt halt. Behind us, a menacing shadow had emerged: the top of Mount Vesuvius had vanished, and a colossal umbrella pine shape of ash had been sent shooting upward, reaching skyward with daunting branches that sprawled sideways and sagged under their own weight. Its color was pale gray, marbled with the brown of the earth it had propelled.

I stood still, my mouth hanging open. This was not a nightmare anymore. All the ominous signs had proven true. Regret washed over me for not having warned anyone. But how could we have known when the day would come?

People poured into the street to gaze at the astonishing spectacle. Screams of terror and chaos ensued. Without a moment to discuss or contemplate, we ran as fast as our legs could carry us, unsure of which direction to take. My father and our pursuers had disappeared amid the mayhem.

An earthquake shook the ground, shattering pottery, breaking columns, and cracking walls. Buildings around us swayed in a perilous dance. The initial ash cloud partially veiled the sky when a second roar followed.

"This is serious!" Basileus said. "Let's head to my house!

"My house is closer from here," Renatus said. "Let's go, run!"

The city had turned into a perilous maze of crumbling buildings and streets cracked open with steaming fissures. Desperate cries filled the air as we maneuvered through the rubble, dodging falling rocks and unstable structures. Every step was a perilous gamble as we tried not to get engulfed by the stampeding crowd.

"Keep running!" I urged my friends.

A colossal black cloud advanced menacingly toward the city, like a roaring waterfall of solid darkness. We kept running through the messy streets, as the air was now thick with acrid smoke and the earth kept trembling beneath our feet. After an eternity, we reached Renatus's home. We knocked frantically, and Gaia opened the door, almost out of breath. "Come inside, quick!"

We rushed in, coughing and retching, as the day was speedily morphing into night.

"It seems that Vulcan is truly angered by the performance," Basileus said.

"This is no time for jokes, Basileus," Renatus said. "Let's hope this stops soon and doesn't cause too much damage."

"I'm afraid that won't happen," Eusebius said. "You read it yourselves; it's all in the scrolls." A few minutes passed in silence as the gravity of the situation dawned upon us. "I want to say one thing," he continued in the most solemn voice I had ever heard from him. "Even in this dark hour, you must understand that this event is merely the outcome of the ceaseless workings of nature, not the will of an imaginary being. Why would Vulcan slay of the devotees who offered him sacrifice?"

"Maybe the sacrifice wasn't enough to appease his fury," Caecilia said.

"Such thoughts are futile, my dear," Eusebius replied. "There are elements that lie dormant for centuries, only to stir at some point in the course of nature, causing great destruction. Nature does not know or care that we are here. She will persist in her transformation, as she has done for ages, heedless of our suffering. Both virtuous and wicked men will meet their end tonight. It is not retribution or the wrath of any god: it is simply change."

We remained silent for a moment.

"But this occurrence won't lead people to think that way," I said. "It will tarnish the reputation of the philosophy for decades to come. And I'm afraid that—" My words were cut short by a frightening rattle of rocks furiously lapidating roofs and windows.

"There's no time to lose," Gaia said, "Leave now!"

"We should all leave," I said.

"No," Eusebius declared, locking eyes with Gaia, and receiving a nod in response. "We will stay. This is our home, and we'll never abandon it."

"But you don't stand a chance," I said. "You'll be buried alive!"

"My husband is right," Gaia said. "We're old and will only slow you down. Besides, adding a year or two to our lives won't contribute to our happiness. Enduring the hardships of flight is worthwhile for you, young ones who still have much joy ahead, but not for us. We would suffer more during the journey than the pleasure we could experience afterward."

The growl of Mount Vesuvius echoed through the air once more. Gaia's eyes widened with a mixture of concern and trepidation.

"Don't argue any longer, go now!" she exclaimed.

Renatus clasped his mother's hands, and with eyes brimming with tears, embraced her warmly. Eusebius ran to the library amid the incessant rattling and returned with a stack of scrolls, which he stuffed in satchels and distributed among us. "These are the essential teachings of the master," he said. "People perish. Books are immortal. Make them known to the world, so it may find happiness. Religion and ignorance have the potential to devastate a civilization even more profoundly than a volcano. But ideas possess the power to resurrect it at any given moment."

"Take this too," Gaia said, hastening into the interior of the house. "Here's enough gold to get you all to Greece. Use it wisely," she said, placing a velvet purse in Renatus's hands. "And use these pillows to shield your heads from the rocks," she added, distributing them between us. "Take my jewelry too," she insisted, removing her necklaces and bracelets, and putting them on Caecilia.

We said our goodbyes exchanging heartfelt hugs. Caecilia held onto Gaia for an extended moment. "Hold back your tears, honey," Gaia said with a smile as they parted. "We'll die content, knowing that you'll find happiness far away."

"You must head to the port," Eusebius said. "The only escape route is by sea." We exchanged glances and nodded. "Take this lamp too," Eusebius added, handing Renatus a small oil lamp and lighting it. "You'll make it. I believe in you," he said, patting his son's cheek.

With a lump in his throat, Renatus vowed, "I promise, Dad."

30

Outside, the ground was now covered with lightweight, sharp-angled rocks up to one foot, and more of them continued to fall steadily. They air felt hot and heavy, reminiscent of the opening of a furnace door. The streets were shrouded in darkness, engulfed by an unnatural night, like a closed room without windows. The ashen cloud, oppressive and suffocating, carried a strong odor of sulfur, making every breath a struggle. With our tunics pulled up to shield our noses and mouths, and the pillows covering our heads, we pressed forward through the dismal chaos. Tension and fear gripped our hearts as the distant rumbling of Mount Vesuvius grew louder and more ominous with each passing moment.

Our lamp flickered weakly, casting only a feeble light in the encroaching darkness, as a tide of humanity was swept up in terror: old men stumbling and falling, their weak legs unable to support them; women crying out in distress, their stained faces etched with anguish; children clinging desperately to their mothers, their eyes wide with fear.

People were aimless, bewildered, demented with grief. Their faces resembled terrifying masks, ash-white and blood-stained. Many collapsed and perished—some suffocated by the dense fumes, others succumbing to their failing hearts, and yet others buried under the weight of collapsing roofs. The city that had once been so lively and vibrant was now a place of agony and dread, swallowed by the fury of the mountain.

We had only managed to walk a few blocks among ruins, overturned carts, and lifeless bodies, when the ground shook, causing Cecilia to lose her balance and fall.

"I sprained my ankle!" she cried out. "Leave me, save yourselves. Run, go!"

"We'll never leave you!" I said to her.

Basileus leaped in front of me and scooped Caecilia into his arms. We resumed our march and sped our pace. Ash and rock kept falling relentlessly like a rain of despair and the throngs of people made the path treacherous. An elderly couple wept beside the road, too exhausted to continue. I understood now why Eusebius and Gaia had refused to join us.

After an agonizing hour, the city walls rose before us. In an attempt to reach the gates, we found ourselves squeezed by the slow walking crowd—many of whom were clutching tightly to their few personal belongings. On the other side, the distant calls of sailors provided a faint glimmer of hope. Hearing that some people were getting into boats to reach the galleys that had come to the rescue, we hurried to the shore.

There we were met with an unsettling sight: the sea had withdrawn, leaving numerous creatures writhing on the sand. We had to tread carefully to avoid slipping as we walked among them. Behind us, in the city, colossal tongues of fire pierced the darkness, seemingly emanating from engulfed houses.

Many implored the gods for help; others cursed them in despair. Some, overcome with fear, prayed for a quick death. The most pessimistic among us declared that the whole world had plunged into its final, everlasting night. And then there were us, the only ones who understood that any chance of salvation depended entirely on our own efforts.

Crammed into a small boat with ten other people, we were able to reach one of the galleys, where sailors hurried us aboard. The ship attempted to leave port amid the rain of cinder, but visibility was reduced to mere feet, and the sea was a shapeless blur between ash and water.

"We're not taking any chances, folks," a sailor cried amid the noise of the waves. "We've got to wait for the wind to change and clear the way, no way we're sailing blind into this rough sea."

Dread and apprehension gripped my heart, but at least now we had distanced ourselves from the quaking earth. The echoing screams of those left behind faded into the ominous backdrop of the erupting volcano, creating an indelible memory. In the unforgiving darkness that enveloped us, my friends and I sought solace in each other's presence, holding tight.

When night fell—or what we could only assume was night—
we huddled in a corner amid the creaking of the ship under
the relentless motion of the strong waves. Our grip tightened
on our scant belongings, especially the invaluable scrolls
bearing the master's teachings. The dwindling oil in our lamp
cast an faint glow, and the sailors' troubled expressions
offered little solace. Sleep was unthinkable.

Yet, human troubles persisted. Some passengers had been
eyeing us suspiciously since we boarded the ship. Taking
advantage of a moment when we had closed our eyes for
respite, a man pilfered one of the scrolls from our packs.

"Look, everyone," he bellowed. "These are the atheists
who dared to desecrate Vulcan's temple! They have brought
the wrath of the gods upon us with their wicked teachings.
They must be cast overboard!" A menacing group closed in
on us. "Now you shall face the fury of mighty Neptune," the
man said, leaping toward Renatus, who promptly reacted by
kicking him down, further fueling his fury.

A watchful sailor stepped forward. "Shut up, you
scoundrels!" he shouted. "These youngsters are not to blame
for Vulcan's wrath. Let's not descend into baseless
accusations."

The mob, however, was growing both in numbers and
fervor. Another man lunged at us, intending to toss Basileus
overboard. The sailor intervened, thwarting the assault, and
seizing the man by the arm. The assailant resisted, but the
sailor subdued him and threw him into the depths.

"Does anyone else want to follow him?" he challenged.
More sailors came to his support. "We're all in this together,

you fools! Attacking innocent youths won't save us. If anyone else wants trouble, step up now and face the consequences."

The crowd dispersed, murmuring among themselves. Trembling, we clutched the scrolls tightly, realizing now more than ever that they were indeed humanity's last hope of not succumbing to ignorance and superstition.

The following morning, my friends and I stood in silence at the gunwale of the ship. The hues of dawn had been replaced by the muted gray of an ash-laden sky, and the world beyond the ship had become a bleak and desolate landscape. The city of Pompeii now lay buried deep in ash like snow, and the diffused silhouette of Mount Vesuvius—that cruel, odious mountain of my nightmares—loomed in the backdrop, a few fumaroles still billowing from its mouth.

How could Gaia and Eusebius have met their end? Tears ran down my face as I wished for a painless demise, finding solace in the cherished memories of a lifetime filled with pleasures.

With her eyes closed, Caecilia whispered a prayer for the dead. Renatus embraced me, and together we mourned not only the loss of his parents but also the end of the city that had been his home. Basileus, with his hands on Caecilia's shoulders, pledged to honor the memory of Pompeii and its people, living as an upstanding citizen in a foreign land.

As a grim acceptance of the irreversible change wrought by nature began to take root within me, a glimmer of hope for what lay ahead emerged in my heart: we were, for the first time, free to pursue our destiny without threats or bounds.

After some time, we turned away from the desolation and headed inside. Our journey was uncertain, but we were more united than ever. As the ship pulled away from the shore, leaving the devastated remains of Pompeii behind, I rejoiced in the company of my most cherished treasure: a newfound family who embraced and loved me for who I was, and to whom I returned the love in kind. The future ahead was a white wall for us to paint our dreams on. A new and exciting life awaited us in the distant land of the Greeks, free from fear and trepidation. We sailed forth, toward freedom.

Epilogue — 1863

A man in a frock and top hat walked among sweat-soaked laborers working tirelessly under the scorching afternoon sun in the hinterland of Campania as they unearthed the colorful walls of half-ruined buildings and the tall columns of ancient temples. Carefully traversing the uneven terrain, he adeptly dodged the swings of picks and shovels, making his way through layers of solidified volcanic ash and rubble. His avid curiosity and scholarly purpose surpassed any discomfort from his refined attire, and he did not hesitate to stop at every corner to examine details of the remains of a city suspended in time.

In the distance, the once majestic silhouette of Mount Vesuvius stood in a shape that would have astonished the inhabitants of Pompeii: its proud cone had crumbled inward into a vast caldera, so that from afar the mighty giant now had the humble form of a hunchback. It too bore the consequences of its actions, doomed to eternal disfigurement.

Stepping into one of the recently excavated structures, the man received a warm welcome from Giuseppe Fiorelli, the worksite supervisor. "Mr. Atkins, we are truly honored by your presence."

The Englishman acknowledged the greeting by tipping his hat and proceeded to walk alongside his host through one of the corridors of the exposed *domus*, with the team of scientists and some workers following behind.

"These are some of the most recent casts created with my process," Fiorelli explained, pointing to the human-like figures lying on both sides. The shapes included a woman cradling her baby, a man writhing in pain, and a dog coiled on a chain. "This cast," he elaborated, pointing to a couple clinging to each other in a tight embrace, "corresponds to a man and a woman, possibly in their forties or fifties. Their posture reflects the poignant display of their enduring love until the final moments. We find it very touching."

"It's truly remarkable," Mr. Atkins expressed. "This is an invaluable gift to humanity. All of them should be featured in an exhibition."

"But what about this one?" Fiorelli asked, pointing to the cast of a man, his right hand with fingers curled over his crotch and his right leg flexed in a relaxed posture, suggesting he had had a more "transcendent" transition compared to his counterparts.

A flush of embarrassment colored Mr. Atkins's face as he attempted to restrain his reaction, but it quickly became apparent that he wouldn't be able to hold it in. He burst out laughing, the sound resonating so loudly that it triggered laughter from some in the vicinity, while others wore expressions of indignation. Mr. Atkins bent over, his stomach aching, and tears streaming from his eyes.

"Good Lord!" he exclaimed when he regained composure. "Well, he certainly met his end on a joyful note," he added with another bout of laughter.

"Surely that's how I want to go," one of the workers commented.

"So it wasn't only Mount Vesuvius that had an eruption that day," the Englishman quipped.

This time no one could contain their laughter.

Printed in Great Britain
by Amazon

49596726R00162